AN EMPTY ACHE

NOVEL 3 IN THE SERIES
SCRAPBOOKS OF THE SOUL

MARILYN HAMMOND, PHD

EMPRESS
PUBLICATIONS
WWW.EMPRESSPUBLICATIONS.COM

SCRAPBOOKS OF THE SOUL

Explore the mesmerizing universe of **Scrapbooks of the Soul**, a compelling series of novels where fiction merges with profound inquiry. Each book is a rich mosaic, filled with diverse fictional characters who delve into the mysteries of the soul, sleeptime dreams, brain hemispheres, and the intersections of spirituality and science. Their dialogues, embellished with insightful footnotes, navigate through themes of whole-brain Christianity, and the intricacies of psychological, generational, and cultural healing.

These stories are more than narratives; they are a reflection on human experience, encompassing long-standing friendships, resilient relationships, and our struggle with life's opposites. The series offers a unique perspective, suggesting our reality is shaped by our perceptions and interpretations. Engage with **Scrapbooks of the Soul** to discover a world where each page mirrors the complexity of life and the varied interpretations that define our existence.

Novel #1 *Deep Hints and Clues*
Novel #2 *What Might We Know*
Novel #3 *An Empty Ache*
Novel #4 *Sit With It*
Novel #5 *Backyard Talk*
Novel #6 *Approach Boldly* (Plus Series Index)

DEDICATION

Loving gratitude to Jay (Trey) for topics of conversation over the years,
and the poem

TABLE OF

CONTENTS

CHAPTER ONE

Deism

On this sunny Saturday morning in Sandshell FL, during the Covid-19 pandemic, Cynthia Kendrick and her father Zach were having breakfast at the kitchen table while Dee was already working in the garden, which was no longer only a flower garden, for the space had been enlarged, gobbling up some of the lawn, and become a vegetable garden after the coronavirus pandemic appeared on the scene.

Dee had heard stories of the 1930s Great Depression from her grandparents, whose stories of financial poverty stuck with her. She could feel fear still alive in them from that hard time as they told their stories, and she internalized what it meant for money to seem to disappear from the pockets of most people—to live in a malfunctioning economy—to worry about where the next meal was coming from.

At the breakfast table Cynthia was sharing with her dad, she remarked, "I heard something vital yesterday on TV about the opposite of faith not being doubt, but certainty, which makes sense to me. For if I know something certainly, faith (trust without proof) need not be part of the picture. For instance, if I know gravity is real, I will not jump from a high building expecting to fly. I know with certainty I will fall to the ground and likely be injured or worse.

"Related to this pandemic, we don't know how long it will last or how many changes will be lasting, we can only trust (have faith) that in the long run, valuable lessons will be learned, culture will change for the better. A healthy culture is one that prescribes (recommends) whatever helps one live well, and proscribes (prohibits) what undermines living well. This is clear in religion where ideas, stories, sayings, rituals or whatever, help humans trust there is a creative source in the universe that cares about each person and prescribes (recommends) trusting in that caring source, while religion also proscribes (prohibits) certain behaviors that go against living well."

Cynthia, the soon-to-become second-grade teacher could be an overbearing lecturer, even to her father, yet he was ever patient with her, as Cynthia continued, "Deism believes a Source created everything, but does not personally intervene in the affairs or efforts of human beings. We are on our own. Which makes me wonder who needs a God like that?"

Zach was preparing to join Dee tending to the garden, but first answered Cynthia's question about who needs a God like that. He suggested, "Maybe someone certain of handling life on their own without the need for a caring, involved God." Cynthia did not immediately respond, as Zach rose from the table, "I am *certain* Dee needs me in the garden," putting his dishes into the dishwasher, but then sitting down again at the table, echoing Cynthia's question, "Who does need a God indifferent to humanity's plight?"

He continued, "Perhaps some folks do well without assuming there is a caring element in the universe. I just don't happen to be one of them. When your mother died, I would never have made it without divine help. I had two children who needed me and a job that needed my focus. I prayed, begged for help, while I grieved, felt bewildered and lost.

"I was raised with the Bible, learned verses of hope that overcome helplessness. In my desperation, things fell into place: a job that gave me time flexibility, Mrs. Arndt for you kids after school and other times. Day by day the situation was doable. I'm glad Dee always sent cards and telephoned Mr. and Mrs. Arndt on their birthdays. They're both gone now. I never understood why Roxanne had to die.

"Some said God needed her more than we did, which I never believed. She had high blood pressure, took medication, which warned she shouldn't mix with alcoholic beverages, and it was determined she died of heart failure. She sometimes drank a moderate bit of wine in the evening, as she had the night she died. Was it the wine with the medication that took her life?"

The kitchen was quiet. Cynthia was looking intently at her dad; perhaps she was looking for tears or some evidence of sorrow, when it occurred to her that she didn't need to satisfy this curiosity about whether her dad still felt sad. Cynthia was aware at that moment that she sometimes gathered evidence to fulfill a need of hers to have secret knowledge about others. Or was she simply trying to validate her hunches?

Cynthia was ever-aware that Monique may have been accurate years ago suggesting Cynthia was dealing with her own powerlessness, needing to have power over others by magnifying their vulnerabilities.

Recently, Cynthia became acquainted with the word, "snide," which, in German has to do with cutting. Snide remarks cut into another. She was increasingly aware that what she labeled her sarcastic side, which she rather approved of, was actually her tendency to make snide remarks that cut into others, embarrassing, humiliating them. Could this be so?

CHAPTER TWO

Need for Divine Love

A Saturday morning at the kitchen table with her dad, Cynthia was able to hold her tongue and allow him to speak without inserting herself into what he was saying or being snide. She could have asked if he was still sad about her mother's death, even though he and Dee had been married a long time. Who did he love more, Roxanne or Dee? Who did he get along with better? With whom did he have better sex?

Cynthia shocked herself with this last question. What was wrong with her? Where did that thought come from? Maybe everyone has thoughts like this, but Cynthia couldn't be sure she wouldn't sometime blurt out this question to her dad. She was appalled at herself; she needed to be more prudent. Why did she have this intrusive, cutting side?

She remembered a fortune-cookie she'd gotten with a statement about the difference between temptation and opportunity. She wasn't sure she understood the difference between the two, but she now saw she had the temptation to ask inappropriate questions and took the opportunity to knock people off-guard, but why did she do that? What did she get out of embarrassing someone, putting them on the spot, so to speak?

Even if, when she was young, she'd felt powerless when her dad and Charles were joking, laughing, teasing, and didn't understand their banter, she need not be governed by feelings of powerlessness now that she was no longer a child. Cynthia was scolding herself.

Sherry, friend from university days, now living in Sandshell, beginning her career as a psychological counselor with Francine, helped Cynthia realize some of her power-plays, for Sherry had the knack to lead someone to the obvious in themselves without burdening or agitating. And Sherry did not fall prey to Cynthia's provocative, cutting observations. Sherry knew the power of quiet. Sherry did not always respond to others' remarks. Cynthia saw that strength in Sherry. Dee did that, too. Sometimes silence speaks loudly. Sherry and Dee both had a talent for peacemaking, Cynthia decided.

Cynthia was again learning about herself that morning in the kitchen, as her father talked about Deism, and his realization that he needed an involved deity, not one remote, distant, unconcerned with human struggle, "If suffering, sacrificial Jesus hadn't come along, we'd still be needing someone like that. Humanity needs help of every kind or we can't make it."

Zach continued, "I believe human love can take us just so far, and then we need divine love. If we don't have a relationship with loving divinity, I think we walk around half-angry all the time, ticked-off nobody loves us enough, though we may never admit that. We then soothe ourselves by finding fault with others to pay them back for not loving us enough, which just makes us more unlikeable. And there you have it!"

Cynthia was impressed with her father's insight, and he seemed to be talking about her without meaning to. Cynthia was learning about self-pity and how pitiful self-pity is. She saw this in herself.

She had a question for her dad, a question not drenched with a snide motive. "Do humans create their personal view of God? A punishing God, a loving God?" Zach didn't answer immediately, but then said, "I suppose one could say humans do that. Each person does that even when sharing the same religious tradition with others. A religious tradition is simply a collective, shared mindset of a tribe, or group of people, which today we would probably label culture. Each culture, in its own geographic place with unique topography, climate, plants and animals, collective experience (history), develops its notion of God.

"Jesus was Jewish, grew up with a Jewish mindset, and then Paul, also Jewish, wrote letters to groups of people in his part of the world, Asia Minor, Greece, even Rome, where he traveled, profoundly explaining the implications of his fellow-Jew Jesus, after Paul himself was radically affected by an experience involving Jesus, which happened after Jesus was no longer on earth, and Paul clarified this extraordinary experience for himself and others, who and what this Messiah personality was about, in the letters he wrote.

"Christianity is all about what this anointed personality brought to earth to change Karma in the universe, seen first through the eyes of Jewish Paul, and then through the writings of Jews Matthew, Mark, John, and Luke who was Greek, who tell versions of oral stories floating around about the God-man Jesus.

"Humans create religion, which doesn't mean religion isn't real." Zach rose from the table and went out to the garden.

The pandemic staying-at-home-together, slowing down the pace of everyday living, was responsible for Zach's unlikely extended conversation with Cynthia. Time itself had changed for the Kendrick household as well as for others. They were amongst the fortunate with enough financial security to not be crazy from worry about paying bills. Zach and Dee were making donations to help those less fortunate at this time. Vegetables from their garden would be shared with homeless shelters. Zach need not share this with Cynthia, for she knew.

CHAPTER THREE

Poem—Pablo

Zach was working from home these days of the Covid-19 pandemic, managing the affordable housing units he was in charge of. Cynthia was living with Zach and Dee this spring semester, putting final touches on her Master's thesis, learning about online teaching, waiting and hoping to start teaching in the Fall with students in a classroom. She hadn't gotten a job as a reading specialist but as a regular 2nd grade teacher in Sandshell at The Merriweather School, grades K-12, offering education using non-traditional methods for students who do not respond well to usual ways of teaching.

She accepted The Merriweather School position after losing the job she'd found in a Kansas City area school district as a reading specialist, due to budgetary concerns related to the pandemic. After first feeling crushed, she then realized she had plenty of reason to be fine with her situation, living at home with Zach and Dee.

For one thing, Cynthia's university friend Sherry was living in Sandshell, continuing to be mentored by Francine with the expectation of taking over Francine's counseling practice when Francine retired. Sherry was polishing her dissertation, expecting to graduate from the university without ceremony because of the Covid-19 sequester. Sherry was living in a wonderful beachside guest apartment Francine found for her, which Cynthia wished was hers. Sometimes Cynthia wished for what others had.

For instance, she sometimes wished for her brother Charles' simple life in Clarksdale KS, which is why she wanted a job in the Kansas City area, to be near Charles, wife Kendal and young son Monty.

Charles seemed to have an ideal life, and have the whole religious-thing figured out—a simple faith as well as a simple day-to-day existence, which was the only way Cynthia could describe what Charles recently wrote for young son Monty. Charles was just a simpler person than herself, Cynthia concluded.

Cynthia's assessment of Charles was confirmed again, in her mind, when she re-read the untitled prayer or poem he wrote to Monty.

When you are young
May you yearn for the life of God
As you grow
May you thrive in the peace of God
When you sleep
May you rest in the presence of God
As you eat
May you taste the sweetness of God
When you listen
May you hear the voice of God
As you talk
May you speak the words of God
When you look
May you see the beauty of God
As you walk
May you follow the way of God
When you choose
May you reflect the will of God
As you learn
May you know the wisdom of God
When you play
May you enjoy the freedom of God
As you laugh
May you share the joy of God
When you work

May you strive for the justice of God
As you use your gifts
May you show the humility of God
When you love
May you receive the love of God
As you forgive
May you feel the compassion of God
When you pray
May you become a prayer of God
As you become old
May you always remain a child of God

Actually, Cynthia wished she could compose something like this. Whether it was a poem or a prayer didn't make much difference, she found what Charles had written exceptional. She wanted to do something extraordinary. She didn't have Charles's uncomplicated faith about God. Perhaps she was a Deist, she concluded once again. But then, who needs such an impersonal deity, she urgently asked herself repeatedly.

She trusted (had faith) Something or Someone created trees, sun, moon, stars, planets, but it is humans who construct houses, plant gardens, and do the work of planet earth. Plants and animals can pretty much survive on planet earth by themselves, but then comes a human who thinks and plans.

Thinking and planning mostly have to do with language. She would be helping second graders on the path to becoming comprehensive readers. While she sometimes wished she could stretch her mind into physics, or architecture, she would be stretching young minds into being able to read so they could become physicists, architects and so on.

Cynthia felt OK about herself as an elementary school teacher, as she put her dishes into the dishwasher that Saturday morning. She didn't expect romance was on the horizon for her in Sandshell, living with her dad and Dee in the house where she grew-up, though glamor-prone Sherry, living beachside, might attract someone, even in quarantine. Such might happen for Sherry. Cynthia now recognized when she was comparing herself to Sherry, who sometimes seemed to live a charmed life, to a degree anyway.

Actually, Cynthia had grown wary of romance last Spring at the university. She no longer thought of her experience as romance. She didn't know what to call it. The attraction started when Cynthia attended the wedding of a friend and met very good-looking Pablo Aguilero, a friend of the groom.

Cynthia and Pablo "clicked," spent the day of the wedding together, danced the evening away, and met for breakfast the next morning before he left for the airport and the flight back to San Antonio TX.

The two had much in common. He was a high school history teacher and baseball coach. They exchanged telephone numbers, e-mail addresses, which put them in constant contact for about a few weeks during which time she shared news about Pablo with Sherry, with her family in Sandshell FL and Clarksdale KS. She recklessly told everyone she was "in love."

Immediately, upon learning about Cynthia's infatuation, Zach was concerned for his daughter for two reasons. First, despite her brash tendencies, he felt she could be taken advantage of. She was a short-sighted thinker who led with her emotions without knowing this about herself.

Second, (and Zach was silently ashamed of this), should this relationship lead to marriage, had she taken into consideration herself having a Latino surname? Having children with a Latino surname? Zach knew as a father he wanted Cynthia to keep her cultural advantages. This was true no matter how bigoted it may be. There were deep prejudices in the land, Zach knew, and was daily reminded in his work with affordable housing.

Zach remembered social prejudice against Catholics when he was young. However, that was different. One didn't "look like a Catholic," except for the costumes priests and nuns wore. (He knew they weren't costumes, he told himself with amusement.) Mingling cultural/racial/ethnic identities is more difficult than modifying costumes. Mixing these identities may be *the* final evolutionary challenge. Zach was struggling.

Zach had been golf friends with African-American Reggie for way many years, scarcely noticing Reggie's darker skin and other characteristics. Why was Zach having this concern with Cynthia? Marriage was quite different from having a golf buddy. There would likely be children and

Zach didn't want his grandchildren to bear the burden of social discrimination.

When Cynthia told Zach and Dee that Pablo stopped telephoning and texting, Zach surmised Pablo was either already married, involved with someone else, or might be struggling with not wanting his heart broken by stepping into a difficult ethnic-cultural situation. Zach shared this with Dee, but not Cynthia.

Dee remarked that despite Zach's growing up with prejudice against Catholics, they'd been married now more than twenty years. He answered, "That's because you're an enlightened Catholic." She pointed out, "You didn't know if I was an enlightened Catholic when you married me." He countered, "I knew you could become an enlightened Catholic with my spiritual coaching." They laughed and shared a hearty hug.

Only a short time had passed when communication between Cynthia and Pablo ended. Everything happened so fast. After days of no communication. Cynthia was able to assess, "I've been duped. Pablo isn't who I thought he was."

And then, Pablo telephoned to confess to Cynthia that already on the day they met at the friends' wedding, he was engaged to a relative living in Mexico. He and his fiancé met when they were adolescents. She'd been adopted by cousins as a newborn and the two met at a family reunion when they were adolescents. Over the years they kept in touch, and then planned to marry.

Pablo said he did not think it necessary to talk about his fiancé the day he met Cynthia. However, he found the day with Cynthia exceptionally enjoyable, which left him with confusion and an unintended deception on his part. He sincerely apologized for not being more forthright at the outset. He apologized for the continuing communication between them. He realized he'd encouraged their continued contact to check-out his feelings, his perspective, for their short time together had been enjoyable, perhaps magical.

Pablo confessed he'd been deceptive, a deception that grew every moment he did not tell Cynthia about his other relationship. He hoped she could forgive his selfish, cowardly way of dealing with this. He said he knew better and should have handled the situation better. He wished Cynthia every possible good fortune. He did not say whether he was still engaged to the other person, but Cynthia said his silence on the matter indicated he was.

His forthright way of dealing with the situation made Cynthia yearn all the more for him. She'd found a guy as solid as her dad and now he was permanently unavailable. Plucky Cynthia decided she'd be smarter in the future. She'd been naïve. She'd ask more questions next time. She wanted to understand what the "magic" she and Pablo seemed to have, was about. And why she still longed to be with this person she scarcely knew.

Cynthia talked at length with Sherry, as friend and budding psychological counselor. She talked on the telephone with brother Charles in Clarksdale. A strange thing happened as Cynthia sought help from Sherry and Charles.

CHAPTER FOUR

Falling in Love

Cynthia felt Sherry and Charles said much the same about what goes on in this whole "falling in love" experience. And then Cynthia came to realize psychotherapist Francine influenced what Sherry said, and so too, Francine had an impact on the views of Charles. Cynthia hadn't known that Charles's senior year in college he was so confused about the thrilling, wondrous, life-changing, energizing, agonizing "being in love" phenomenon that could wreck one mentally/emotionally when the relationship ended, that he got a job with a retail department store to pay for telephone sessions with Francine to help him understand the power, passion and devastation of "being in love."

Of course, Sherry was still struggling with romance and relationship herself, whereas Charles and Kendal seemed quite content with each other and especially with little son Monty. Cynthia knew before meeting Pablo that "in-loveness" didn't guarantee a fulfilling, lasting relationship. Look at the divorce rate in culture, when probably most couples marry because they're "in love." She knew the thrill of romantic attraction often ended badly. Cynthia thought about dad Zach. Had he truly fallen in love with both Roxanne and Dee? She wanted to ask him. Why did she hesitate? She would likely one day ask him. She now struggled with asking questions that violated other peoples' privacy.

From Sherry and Charles, Cynthia gathered Francine's questions and impressions about romantic attraction. It seems psychotherapist Francine didn't find romantic attraction to be about love, and therefore did not speak of romantic love, only romantic attraction. However, Francine respected romantic attraction as real, worth trying to understand, for it says something about us psychologically, and perhaps spiritually.

In romantic attraction, something about another person jumps out at us, so to speak. We are inexplicably drawn to someone or something, but why? Why this appeal that stirs us emotionally? Why had Cynthia and Pablo had this mutual experience?

Cynthia gathered from Sherry and Charles questions and impressions that Francine held, which helped one think about what is going on when romantic attraction happens. Cynthia summarized their views gathered from Francine: (1) Romantic attraction is an opportunity to learn something important about oneself, one's life, through another's traits, characteristics, qualities, life circumstances. (2) If romantic attraction is a chemical reaction, such as hormones going wild, what triggers the chemicals? (3) Gain perspective by using the phrase "being-in-attraction" rather than "being-in-love." (4) Don't forget sexual attraction is part of our nature. Try to be clear about the difference between psychological attraction and sexual attraction. (5) Do you tend to "fall in love" with a particular type of person, perhaps your opposite personality type? (6) Have you ever been "in love" with someone you didn't like, which can be a prime time to learn something about yourself. Liking and "being in love" can be different.

Francine used the phrase "being-in-love" to express ultimate human fulfillment as a human being in love with Being; total Being; the Beingness of the universe. Further, she interpreted romantic attractions as snippets of meeting unknown aspects of our being, recognizing something(s) about our being with the other person inadvertently playing the role of a psychological mirror, wherein we learn about who we are and what we might contribute to Life.

Quite simply, we "fall in love" with aspects of our own being, which is why we feel torn asunder when the relationship breaks up, as if we are losing aspects of our very existence; so great is the pain we feel we cannot live without the other person.

Francine talked about human longing for Love, as religion at its best embodies. Being connected to Divine Love roots us in our own being. Christian mystics have used the phrase "Union with God" to talk about experiencing Being. In romantic attraction one is introduced to aspects of one's own being in extraordinary ways, feeling intensely alive and energized, though it may take years to figure out what was revealing itself.

Romantic attraction is an opportunity to learn about one's being. However, the more intense the attraction, the less likely a lasting relationship will be established, Francine was convinced. If looking for an enduring relationship, "liking" each other is more important. "Liking" is the soil in which love can grow. These were some of Francine's ideas about so-called "romantic love."

Charles told Cynthia about his attraction in college to the movie *Of Gods and Men,* based on the true story of eight French Trappist monks living in a poor community in Algeria, having to decide during the Algerian Civil War under threat by fundamentalist terrorists, whether to stay in Algeria and possibly be killed or return to the safety of France. The movie stuck with Charles, who viewed it again and again.

What drew him to this film? What was its attraction? Charles said, "I wasn't Catholic, not interested in becoming a monk or living a celibate life, or risking myself in some heroic way for others. Why did this film attract me?"

"I played with words. Knew I was intrigued, fascinated, captivated, enthralled, enchanted by the movie. The word *enchanted* resonated. The monks *chanting* in the film was my attraction. I began listening to recorded chanting, and this is why the glass hut on the property Kendal and I have fits perfectly as a place I can chant."

Cynthia was impressed with Charles' story about the movie and his chanting. She hoped one day for him to say more about his attraction, his marriage with Kendal. How did the two of them come to their decision to marry? She sometimes daydreamed Pablo would break off his engagement, and they would one day be together.

CHAPTER FIVE

Powerlessness

Cynthia ardently believed most people want a lifelong partner. She didn't know where that came from, unless it was from the death of her mother when Cynthia was young, and living without a mother-figure for three years before Dee entered her life. Or maybe wanting a lifelong partner is just normal, Cynthia told herself.

Cynthia talked most easily with Sherry, soon-to-be Dr. Sherry Gates, caught in the pandemic like everyone else, hoping to build her psychological counselling practice while Francine was phasing out her career as a retiring psychotherapist.

Cynthia and Sherry texted and telephoned often. Each needed conversation that would not be repeated to anybody. Sherry had the tension of living in Sandshell wanting to trust Cynthia could keep strict confidence while aware that Cynthia was prone to blurting out whatever came to mind. Therefore, Sherry was careful what she shared with Cynthia, while Cynthia had the luxury of being confident Sherry would not repeat what Cynthia told her.

Cynthia was continuing her talk about Deism with Sherry on Sherry's beachside balcony one Sunday at lunch. Francine acquired this exquisite apartment for Sherry, an upstairs guest apartment in the large beach home of the grateful parents of a client who felt Francine had helped their troubled daughter tremendously. Out of gratitude, the parents offered the guest apartment to Francine for her use or those of her guests. When Francine inquired if it might be Sherry's apartment for an extended stay for a nominal fee, they easily agreed.

The topic of Deism between Cynthia and Sherry on the balcony led to familiar sayings: "God helps those who help themselves," "Where there's a will, there's a way," contrasted with "Let go and let God." The friends concluded the first two slogans advocate self-sufficiency, whereas "Let go and let God," an anchor in Alcoholics Anonymous, is the opposite.

Sherry was working with clients struggling with drug addiction and was seeing first-hand that recognizing one's powerlessness while letting go and letting God is important in recovery. Cynthia absorbed what Sherry was saying about the power of acknowledging one's powerlessness overcoming addiction and asking one's Higher Power to help.

Cynthia decided then and there, that bright lovely day on the balcony to try the powerless-Higher Power formula in her own life, with her tendency, now lessened but still present, to burst forth with cutting comments. She no longer wanted to even be tempted to blurt out demeaning comments.

At the same time, Cynthia had a memory of Dee turning a bible saying on its head. Instead of Jesus saying "Without Me, you can do nothing," Dee restated, "Without You, I can do nothing."

Cynthia shared this memory with Sherry, who, knowing lots of bible verses said, "That's in the Gospel of John," looked it up on her smart phone and announced, "Yes, Jesus is said to have said, 'Without me you can do nothing' according to John 15:5."

Cynthia was concerned, "How can that saying be reconciled with 'God helps those who help themselves,' and 'Where there's a will, there's a way,' Sherry reflected, "I'd say each adage can be beneficial under different circumstances. These two sayings are not in the bible so far as I know."

Sherry's comment reminded Cynthia of sidewalk professor Oriana's recent shared quote, 'Science and religion do not have to be incompatible: One need not be wrong for the other to be right," which Dee shared with Zach and Cynthia, and made Cynthia wonder, *why do I have negative feelings about Dee, when she shares valuable information, has always been good, kind, and helpful? It's as if I am still a young kid, resentful of her while also knowing she is on my side, from the very beginning, on that first Christmas Day when there was a sandstorm, and she took off her hooded jacket, tied the sleeves around my waist, with the back of the jacket hanging down from my waist shielding my bare legs from the stings of the blowing sand. My negative feelings toward Dee need to stop,* Cynthia told herself.

Amazingly, thereafter Cynthia found herself spontaneously addressing Dee as Mum-Dee, using Charles' pet name for Dee. At the same time, Cynthia started reading biographies and autobiographies, which she found a most enjoyable way to spend the stay-at-home pandemic while putting finishing touches on her Master's thesis.

CHAPTER SIX

Heroines to Cynthia

At the present moment, Cynthia was reading about Simone Weil (pronounced Vay in French), considered a mystic, who died in 1943 at the age of 34, having died of self-imposed starvation and tuberculosis.

Cynthia found herself uncommonly drawn to this intellectually brilliant French female, who was passionate about the suffering of humanity from the time she was a child, who became a philosopher, a teacher of children who taught them philosophy rather than the usual curriculum. Weil became a political activist, advocate for workers, working on an assembly line in a factory for a short while herself, to learn what it was like to be such a worker.

Weil, who was Jewish, became a follower of Christ after extraordinary experiences, though never baptized, she is often regarded a Christian mystic. She suffered with migraine headaches and while having a migraine at a Benedictine abbey in 1938 in France, during Easter week, she found joy in Gregorian chant at the abbey, which has been expressed as an experience of divine love in the midst of affliction, "Christ himself came down and took possession of me." She had had intimate encounters with Christ before, but this time, it is said, "the passion of Christ entered into [her] being once and for all." (*Waiting for God*, 1966, translated 2009, pp. 26, 27).

Cynthia was struck by the impact of Gregorian chant in the life of Weil, and in the life of brother Charles whose home and property with wife Kendal has a glass hut nestled in the midst of a small gathering of trees on the property, built for one man's whittling wood, which became Charles's enchanting place to chant.

Cynthia interpreted the wee-glass structure on the property in Clarksdale, a synchronicity in Charles's life, and was grateful she understood the word synchronicity as those times when situations fall into place; come together in remarkably unlikely, meaningful ways. Cynthia wondered whether her stumbling onto information that Gregorian chant was vital to Weil just as it is to Charles, fits the characteristic of a synchronistic happening in Cynthia's own life. What was Cynthia to make of this? Perhaps Cynthia wasn't a Deist after all. The very idea of synchronicity made her feel that whatever else God might be, there is an intimately caring factor going in the universe, in the daily synchronistic lives of humanity.

Cynthia continued learning about Simone Weil and was not put off by the peculiarities of Weil's excessive passions, or her unique understanding of the relationship between human and God. For instance, in Weil's analogy:

"Two prisoners whose cells adjoin communicate with each other by knocking on the wall. The wall is the thing which separates them but it is also their means of communication. It is the same with us and God. Every separation is a link." (*Gravity and Grace,* 1947, translated 2004, p. 145). Cynthia was drawn to Weil's brilliant and independent mindset, fierce passion, and courageous approach to living out her convictions.

And then, Cynthia re-read the story of Sylvia Ashton Warner, a woman whose teaching technique influenced Cynthia into becoming a teacher. Cynthia was introduced to this woman in a career class in high school, where she learned that this teacher of English heritage, born in New Zealand became a teacher of the young for a number of years (1938-1954), including indigenous Maori children unable to learn to read using British methods, so she devised her own way, having each child build their own set of words by telling her every morning a word they wanted to know, which she spelled out as she wrote the word on a card given to them to go in their own vocabulary file. The children remembered "their" words because the words were meaningful to them, came out of their own experience, and thus they built their own vocabulary and learned to read.

Cynthia admired this teacher's unorthodox method. She saw the teacher's approach as intuitively innovative in contrast to a pre-pared sequential process. Cynthia learned about this pioneering teacher in her high school career class, and at nearly the same time she was introduced to brain-hemisphere differences Francine talked about on the Kendrick patio, and felt the teacher's technique was somehow tied to Francine's brain information. Later, she surmised the pre-pared method was more left-brain, and the teacher's method more right-brain, aware we do not have two brains, but this is simply an abbreviated way of speaking.

Cynthia realized the teacher, Sylvia Ashton Warner was eccentric, even in the way she wrote her book, *Teacher* (1963). The New Zealand teacher followed her own path. Cynthia wanted to do that, and as she observed during this stay-at-home time, Dee was her own person, a centered individual, not eccentric.

Dee planted a vegetable garden before Cynthia heard of others doing such. Further, Dee had researched and written about St. Francis, and was just now explicating the parables of Jesus using an old fourfold way of reading the bible. Dee's work came from her own interior inspiration. She followed her own path, not needing to impress others, but impacting them as a by-product of living well herself. Cynthia wished she could keep admiration for Dee utmost in her mind. However . . .

CHAPTER SEVEN

Transgender Dynamics

One morning, Cynthia awakened from a night of fine sleep with words vividly apparent to her, "An ounce of prevention is worth a pound of cure." She felt sure she'd heard the phrase at some time past, but wondered why no public official she was aware of used the adage during this Covid-19 pandemic. She mentioned the sage-saying to Dee, as well as her concern that she'd not heard any public official utter its wisdom to encourage the current mask-wearing, stay-at-home, social-distancing advice and practices.

Dee recognized the quote, "Benjamin Franklin said those words regarding fire safety, but they certainly apply now, don't they, wearing masks and all the recommendations to limit the spread of the virus." The two talked about the current need for data, graphs, statistics, numbers, to tell of virus cases, deaths, economic repercussions, while media also reported stories of the personal toll of the virus on individuals, families.

Dee innocently remarked, "I wonder why those words came to you."

Cynthia's not-yet fully-tamed acid tongue spewed, "And why wouldn't or shouldn't the words come to me?" followed immediately by, "I'm sorry. Apparently, your knowing this was a Benjamin Franklin quote triggered my feeling of powerlessness; my fear of never being well-informed compared to you having all kinds of information at your fingertips."

Remarkably unflustered Dee merely observed, "I've had years to acquire tidbits of this and that, because of loving to read, which may have been a substitute for relating to others, even relating to myself." And then she added, "The older I grow, the more I know what I don't know."

Cynthia was grateful that Dee was a genuine person with an inquiring mind who'd put together those summertime dinners on the Kendrick patio featuring Francine. Cynthia cherished those gatherings on the patio that summer, which may have helped moderate somewhat her adolescent arrogance of believing she knew more than she did at the time. She realized she still had a "know it all" attitude, despite admiring Dee's inquiring mind, and dad-Zach's interest in the Great Courses when she was young, as well as his many-faceted interests now.

Lately, Cynthia had come to entertain the possibility that her dad saw exceptional intellectual curiosity in Dee, which attracted him to her; was a mirror of his own intellectual curiosity. And maybe he was attracted to Dee's fierce independence, being true to herself, understanding herself.

Recently, now that Dee and Cynthia had more time to talk between the two of them during this pandemic, Dee had begun revealing her long-time gender-confusion to Cynthia, and the series of happenings that helped her struggle through and beyond the confusion.

Dee related the origins of her gender-confusion as she now understood them. Her immature father's fear about having weak children, rooted in the death of his baby sister Agnes, when he himself was very young. The need for Dee's father Harold, whom Cynthia had come to call grandpa-Harold, to name his children after prizefighters. Dempsey's over-identification with masculine qualities in herself while devaluing the feminine. Dempsey's young mother's need to acquiesce to the immaturities of her young husband.

Then there was young Dempsey's admiration of Aunt Tess. Cynthia remembered Aunt Tess as the sick woman who wore turbans, the woman who lived with Dempsey, who died in Florida after coming to Florida to get well.

Dee shared with Cynthia the influence of Aunt Tess on Dempsey after Dempsey moved to Stamford, and how Tess's cancer diagnosis accelerated Dempsey's role as caregiver, which began to shift personality dynamics in Dempsey. Dee told Cynthia, how, in Florida, the Kendrick family had its impact on Dempsey's identity, and most especially, Zach's attraction to Dempsey, and finally the breakthrough metaphoric understanding of Dempsey about herself with Ann Dramm helping explicate the purple aura cat vision, followed by Dempsey legally changing her name from Dempsey to Dee.

Cynthia and Dee talked at length about the split-brain understanding of Francine with her mobius band on the Kendrick patio, which solidified and helped further heal Dee's gender-confusion. Thus, Cynthia came to have a rough outline of Dee's gender-crisis and its resolution, which Dee reiterated, "This is my story; my story alone. Each person's story is uniquely theirs."

Dee voiced gratitude that physical gender transition was not yet fully popularized during her years of gender struggle. Dee felt indeed fortunate, "Psychological factors were uncovered rather than my choosing to have physical components medically, surgically altered to solve my dilemma. Psychological understanding resolved my confusion rather than physiological interpretation, explanation, treatment."

Dee's words rang a bell with Cynthia: "Psychological rather than physiological interpretation." Cynthia had long been familiar with the importance of how we interpret the world we live in, including our experiences. She knew Dee's focus on Francis of Assisi had to do with his habits of interpretation, and Dee's work with Jesus' parables was all about interpretation; how we relate to them based on our interpretation or someone else's interpretation.

How could Cynthia not know about the importance of interpretation, practical hermeneutics, the meanings humans extract from or put into and onto internal and external experience. Cynthia felt smart at the moment. And what was Dee's current project? Something about hermeneutics, Cynthia felt certain, as she wondered whether Zach knew about Dee's transgender struggle.

CHAPTER EIGHT

Soothsaying

Cynthia's acquaintance with the topic of interpretation (hermeneutics) was a bridge in her friendship with Sherry. Well actually, Francine was the bridge in the relationship. The two friends recently talked about two categories of acquiring knowledge in German idealist philosophy because Francine had mentioned this to Sherry. One category, was called 'natural sciences' which gathers data, and replicates results when appropriate. The second category is to pay attention to single events which cannot be replicated, labeled 'sciences of the spirit.'

Sherry elaborated, "Every person's story in psychological counseling falls in the category 'science of the spirit,' for each story is unique. While there are similar themes between stories, no two persons have exactly the same story. Every day, I marvel at this as I listen to individual stories."

Cynthia felt on par with Sherry in this discussion as Sherry seemed to assume Cynthia was already acquainted with Francine's information through Dee. This wasn't the case, though Cynthia never corrected Sherry in her assumptions that Cynthia had been exposed to Francine's knowledge.

Sherry chuckled about the German words for the distinction between these two kinds of inquiry and knowing: "Both are labeled *Wissenschaften* (sciences) in German. "Natural sciences" do research, gather data, use mathematics, replication and prediction, and are labeled *Naturwissenschaften*.

"Sciences of the spirit" are history, literature, philosophy, theology, the fine arts and such, named *Geisteswissenschaften*. I thought you'd want to know this."

They laughed, as Cynthia commented humorously, "I've always wanted to know this," followed by, "But seriously, Francine is an exceptionally knowledgeable person." To which Sherry replied, "And I am forever grateful to you for my connection with her."

Whereupon Cynthia wondered if Francine knew Dee's transgender story, triggered by Dee's comment that this was her personal story alone. Cynthia was tempted to tell Sherry Dee's story, but did not do so, vividly aware it was not her story to tell. Cynthia felt a personal victory over her temptation to tell too much which she knew was a cheap way to make her look like she knew a great deal of whatever. Cynthia saw this tendency of hers as part of her *shadow*, a term she learned from Sherry.

Psychologically, every person has a shadow which are traits the individual is partly or completely in the dark about, speaking metaphorically, unaware of, even unlived positive elements, which Dee explained about herself, "I had a strong streak of independence in me which didn't know how to live in the outer world, except as stubbornness."

Cynthia still wondered why the Benjamin Franklin quote had come to her, embarrassed to mention it again to Dee after botching the earlier opportunity, but sharing her question about Franklin's quote with Sherry, hoping for a spurt of insight from Sherry, which didn't happen.

Sherry was presently happy about a telephone conversation with Justin, Monique's son, whom Sherry met at the Kendricks at Christmas. Sherry told Cynthia, "He called; I was thrilled and said so. We caught up with what was going on in our pandemic lives." Sherry didn't reveal more about talking with Justin, except to say they planned to meet at a restaurant as soon as such re-opened after the coronavirus restrictions lifted.

Their telephone conversation had been lengthy, with Justin saying he'd wanted to contact Sherry but felt he first needed to get some things *straight* with himself. He emphasized the word *straight* and they both laughed. Humor seemed a natural reaction to his inuendo. Justin had a sly sense of humor.

In the last seconds of their conversation, Justin suggested he come see Sherry and her beachside living quarters, to which she easily agreed.

In a few days, late afternoon on Saturday, looking hale, hearty, healthy with his face mask on, he arrived at Sherry's door, the door opening to reveal her wholesome sheen of glamour obvious despite the face mask she was wearing.

After a quick walk-through of the small apartment, they were on the balcony with Justin saying seriously, yet also in jest, "Someday I hope to own a seaside villa like this," And then they talked for some time, adjusting their seating with the large table umbrella on the tiny terrace, as the bright sun moved ever west and became eventual sunset.

They started with iced water and graduated to wine and varying hors d'oeuvres as the evening progressed. Covid-19 gave them plenty to talk about. Previously, Justin brought up his comment to Monique, "For all you know I may be gay" to discourage his mother from needling him about marriage and grandchildren. He did so again this evening. He also mentioned mother Monique's garbled talk about right-brain, left-brain from Brunch Bunch gatherings, and said he wished he understood "this brain-hemisphere stuff."

Perhaps intuition prepared for this Saturday time together. At any rate, Sherry had brought from Francine's office a mobius band Francine created to demonstrate split-brain differences, as well as a file of Francine notes. On the outside of the folder, Francine had written, *Soul, Split-Brain, Etc.* Sherry read aloud from a note card: "John Sanford (1929-2005), Episcopal priest and Jungian analyst (depth psychologist) states:"

> The soul today is an orphan . . . It seems unforgivable that the Church should have abandoned soul, since soul looms so large in the Sacred Scriptures on which the Church is founded. . . The early Church Fathers honored soul. They wrote treatises on the soul, and on dreams . . . and often they sounded like depth psychologists rather than theologians.[1]

Justin asked, "And exactly what's a depth psychologist?" which Sherry briefly answered by reminding him, "We once talked about children carrying the burden of the unlived life of their parent, which is

---

[1]John A. Sanford, *The Kingdom Within: The Inner Meaning of Jesus' Sayings,* (New York NY: Harper & Row, 1970, 1987) p. 118.

psychological aspects that are unknown, unrealized, underdeveloped or undeveloped potential in their parents. The Swiss psychiatrist (soul doctor) who wrote of this child-parent connection was Carl Jung, a pioneer in depth psychology."

She rifled through papers in the folder, found the one she wanted, and handed it to Justin, "This summarizes the focus of depth psychology and makes powerful allusions to brain-hemisphere differences. The author of these remarks is not regarded a depth psychologist, whereas Sigmund Freud and Carl Jung are pioneers in depth psychology which goes below the surface of the personality, deals with what we don't know about ourself; what we're unaware of. Perhaps it's not far-fetched to say depth psychology is more interested in right-hemisphere knowings.

Sherry handed Justin a piece of paper from Francine's folder on which Francine had written, "Freud's *Interpretation of Dreams* was published in 1902, same year as William James's book, *Varieties of Religious Experience*. Justin read Francine's comments.

"Nearly sixty years before split-brain surgeries, American psychologist William James (1842-1910) surmised the different ways in which the brain-hemispheres function. In his 1902 book, , William James spoke of religious experience being related to the B-region (right-hemisphere) of the personality in contrast to A-region which he described as full sunlit consciousness (left-hemisphere). This sounds like *yin* and *yang*.

"Psychologist James said the B-region is the larger part of us. In the B-region everything is implicit, latent, includes all we are not aware of at the moment, such as old memories. B-region also includes obscure likely unnamed longings, impulses, intuitions—insights that come to us, occur out of nowhere, such as phantasies and moods that seem to have a life of their own, like sleeptime dreams and mystical experiences. People naturally drawn to religion are perhaps quite connected to this side of their being."

"So what are split-brain surgeries?" Justin asked, though he had a vague idea. Sherry had a ready answer, "In the 1960s, it was documented that each side of the brain makes distinct contributions to life and living. This information became obvious following surgical research by Nobel Prize-winning neuroscientist Roger Sperry and colleagues at California Institute of Technology, in Pasadena CA.

"At that time, to bring relief to people suffering from uncontrollable epileptic seizures, the two hemispheres of the brain were surgically disconnected by cutting fibers in the corpus callosum which connects the two sides of the brain. This type of surgery is rare today as most seizures can be controlled with medicines.

"After a split-brain surgery, there were investigations into how a patient's personality changed because the two hemispheres of the brain had been surgically disconnected. It began to be clear that having a split-brain changed what patients could and couldn't do. Thus, the differences between left and right brain hemisphere traits, qualities, functions, processes, attitudes, approaches, began to be clearly observed, documented, and written about—and sometimes over-simplified. Also, people who had strokes or brain injuries were studied to learn what they could or could no longer do based on which hemisphere the stroke or injury took place."

Justin nodded, "So much for the split-brain," pointing his finger at the William James paper, "And now for this man with two first names who was guessing about brain-hemispheres before split-brain research. How correct was he?"

Sherry assessed, "I'd say he's quite accurate, beginning with his observation that the B-region (right-hemisphere) is the larger part of each of us in scope and impact.

"Francine talked about what William James describes as "non-rational operations" is what depth psychology deals with, such as sleeptime dreams, emotions roaming around in us, insights, spontaneous phantasies, cravings, impulses, unnamed longings.

"Interestingly, pioneer psychologist William James from the U.S., and depth psychologist Carl Jung from Switzerland did meet, and might have become psychological collaborators but James was thirty-three years older than Jung, so this didn't happen. William James died before such collaboration could progress."

Justin backtracked, "As for the church fathers the Episcopal priest claimed were more in touch with the soul—what is he saying?"

Sherry again rifled through papers in the folder until she found the title of the book that helped answer that question, *God, Dreams, and Revelation: A Christian Interpretation of Dreams* by Morton T. Kelsey (1917-2001), a friend of John Sanford, and like Sanford, an Episcopal priest trained in Jung's psychology.

"Kelsey's book names those in the early centuries of Christianity and their high regard for dreams. Kelsey also includes an important bible translation error by one of the church fathers, St. Jerome." Sherry read:

> In translating Leviticus 19:26 and Deuteronomy 18:10 with one word different from other passages . . . Jerome turned the law: ' You shall not practice augury or witchcraft (i.e., soothsaying) into the prohibition: You shall not practice augury nor observe dreams.' Thus by the authority of the Vulgate [version of the bible used for generations], dreams were classed with soothsaying, the practice of listening to them with other superstitious ideas. [2]

Justin listened, blinked, seemed to understand, "My mom has brought the term "inner world" home from the Brunch Bunch. Inner world is like soul?" Sherry thought a second, "Perhaps. Yes, inner world is everything that goes on inside us—what we are and are not aware of." She was impressed with Justin's attention, his comprehension, his apparent interest in the conversation.

---

[2] Morton T. Kelsey *God, Dreams, and Revelation: A Christian Interpretation of Dreams*, (Augsburg Publishing House, Minneapolis MN, 1968, 1974), p. 155.

CHAPTER NINE

Split-Brain

Sherry continued, "I find the person who tells the split-brain story unbelievably well, is British psychiatrist, Iain McGilchrist, who says human choice creates what seems to be a competition between brain hemispheres, wherein one side can dominate. He claims, in western culture in recent centuries, left-hemisphere traits and qualities have come to be preferred. The left-hemisphere has a narrow focus. The left-hemisphere processes analytically, takes things apart, controls, verifies. The right-hemisphere which sees the whole picture, is intuitive, synthesizes, grasps the overview, and has been de-valued in recent centuries."

Francine had written: "Ideally, the two sides of the brain, work together like dance partners moving in rhythm and harmony. In those with a healthy brain, whose corpus callosum has not been severed, both sides of the brain work in tandem. Both sides are necessary. Yet we do have cultural preferences and habits about which brain processes we value and depend upon most often to make our way through this life.

"Prior to psychiatry, McGilchrist taught English at Oxford University. In the 2009 edition of his book, which took him twenty years to complete (new edition, 2019), he looks at philosophy, art, literature, music, history, metaphor, to make his case that left-brain hemisphere traits have become increasingly dominant in shaping western culture. It seems to me, his two-career background (humanities and psychiatry) makes his book possible. McGilchrist writes:

> My thesis is that for us as human beings there are two fundamen-
> tally opposed realities, two different modes of experience; that
> each is of ultimate importance in bringing about the recognizably
> human world; and that their difference is rooted in the bi-hemi-
> spheric structure of the brain. It follows that the hemispheres
> need to co-operate, but I believe they are in fact involved in a
> sort of power struggle, and that this explains many aspects of
> contemporary Western culture.[3]

Sherry clarified, "McGilchrist claims, in western culture over centuries, the left-brain which processes analytically (by breaking into parts),
deals with what can be verified and validated (scientifically), has come to
dominate; western culture has become lopsided."

Justin remarked, "Which is fascinating. Monique brings bits-and-
pieces from the Brunch Bunch; however, it is garbled and incoherent
when she attempts to explain it."

Sherry took another piece of paper from Francine's folder in which
Francine had written: "Ten years before McGilchrist's book, the late
Leonard Shlain (1938-2009), chief of laparoscopic surgery at California
Medical Center in San Francisco wrote a book on brain-hemisphere
choices and the creation of culture, wherein he tracked how left-hemisphere brain preference grew as literacy (the alphabet) came to dominate
western culture, and concluded that right-hemisphere tendencies are being recovered in U.S. culture today. Shlain concluded:

> I am convinced we are entering a new Golden Age—one in
> which the right-hemispheric values . . . will begin to ameliorate
> the conditions that have prevailed for the too-long period during
> which left-hemispheric values were dominant[4] . . . Of the twin

---

[3] Iain McGilchrist, *The Master and his Emissary: The Divided Brain and the Making of the Western World* (New Haven CT: Yale University Press, 2009), p. 3.

[4] Leonard Shlain, *The Alphabet Versus the Goddess: The Conflict Between Word and Image,* (Viking: New York NY, 1998), p. 432.

human hemispheres, the right side is the elder sibling. In utero, the right lobe of a human fetus's brain is well on its way to maturation before the left side begins to develop.[5]

Sherry explained, "A major contribution of the left side of the brain is language. Shlain, as a vascular surgeon operating on carotid arteries that supply blood to the brain, wrote about the effect of language on brain development:

> I have had the opportunity to observe firsthand the profoundly different functions performed by each of the brain's hemispheres ...We know that in the developing brain of a child, differing kinds of learning will strengthen some neuronal pathways and weaken others ...When a critical mass of people within a society acquire literacy, especially alphabet literacy, left hemispheric modes of thought are reinforced at the expense of right hemispheric ones.[6]

Sherry elaborated, "Shlain's thesis is that as more and more people acquired alphabet literacy the outcome was that alphabet culture was "ladled" into a baby's brain, and the alphabet determined which neuronal pathways of the child's developing brain would be reinforced. He believed our alphabet literacy lopsidedness is correcting itself because of the images, the pictures from television, videos, and movies.

"He also noted that two-hand typing instead of one-hand writing has brought brain preference changes. The computer "mouse" causes hand-eye coordination which is more spatial than linear, and invites right-brain pattern skills in generating the written word. Technology is changing the way we use our brains."

Sherry summarized that the right-hemisphere has traditionally been labeled the minor, inferior side of the brain with fewer mental capacities, contributing little. However, studying stroke victims, those with brain injuries, and surgical split-brain individuals has changed the view of right-hemisphere contributions.

---

[5] Shlain, *The Alphabet Versus the Goddess,* p. 18.
[6] Shlain, *The Alphabet Versus the Goddess,* p. viii.

"What McGilchrist shows magnificently in his book is the importance, indeed the greater influence of the right-hemisphere over the left-hemisphere. He clearly outlines Western culture's lopsided preference in recent centuries for what the left-hemisphere does.

"McGilchrist says the right-hemisphere is more in tune, more grounded, in that which is implicit, subtle, ambiguous. The left-hemisphere is adept at making explicit the implicit, bringing clarity and certainty to what is subtle and ambiguous. However, the downside of the left-hemisphere's talent is that it tends to champion only the clear and certain (what it knows) and its articulation of what it clear and certain (from its viewpoint). Thus, a left-brain dominated culture (or person) may arrogantly over-simplify, limit, constrict, be blinded by its narrowed focus regarding the vastness of life and living, and therefore give simplistic answers to complex questions.

"McGilchrist says all that is "new" or "other" comes from the right-hemisphere. The left-hemisphere acting alone can create only "novelty," and novelty leads to dissatisfaction, to boredom, which leads to a vicious cycle of emptiness and restlessness on the one hand and gross stimulation and sensationalism on the other.

"McGilchrist makes it clear that what actually happens is that whole understanding begins and ends in the intuitive right-hemisphere, the hemisphere that used to be thought of little value. First, there is right-hemisphere intuition. Then, an analysis of a situation by left-hemisphere language. However, analysis alone can become empty; a paralysis of analysis, resulting in restless dissatisfaction and boredom which seeks gross stimulation and sensationalism. Real understanding requires that analysis return to the big picture, the whole view of the right-hemisphere where there is an expansion not only of knowledge or information, but of true understanding out of which can flow something closer to wisdom.

"The process goes like this: Every possibility begins as right-hemisphere intuition, becomes left-hemisphere focused analysis, which then returns to the big picture of the right-hemisphere where new intuitions can be born. McGilchrist claims the dilemma in recent centuries in the Western world has been:

The left hemisphere thinks that it is in control . . . while the reality is that it is selecting from a broader world that has already been brought into being for it by the right hemisphere.[7] . . It is with the right hemisphere that we understand the moral of a story, as well as the point of a joke . . . [the right hemisphere] is particularly important wherever non-literal meaning [like metaphor] needs to be understood.[8]

Francine had added in her notes: "McGilchrist is saying Western culture has been painting itself into a corner. I believe this means, in the East-West split in Christianity since 1054, there has been a tendency in the West of Christianity for right-brain mystical, symbolic, experiential spirituality, to be overrun by doctrine and dogma. Overall, Western culture increasingly has been relying on left-hemisphere traits, devolving into too much analytical rationality. Which has devolved into literal understanding becoming too small for the complexities of life; clarity at the expense of fuller comprehension which includes ambiguity; quantification that too often dismisses what cannot be measured. Overvaluing left-hemisphere contributions has truncated, constricted, brought forth inadequate ways of interpreting life and living. This is now perhaps changing. However, change isn't easy, smooth, or without turmoil."

---

[7] McGilchrist, *The Master and His Emissary*, 2009, p. 191.
[8] McGilchrist, *The Master and His Emissary*, 2009. pp, 70, 71.

CHAPTER TEN

Whole-Brain Functioning

Justin repeated, "Rational limitations; the literal too small for life's complexities; clarity over ambiguity, dismissive quantification, inadequate ways of understanding. If Francine is correct, we are screwed-up, aren't we?"

Also in the folder, Francine had put Carl Jung quotes from his autobiography:

> Most people identify themselves almost exclusively with their consciousness, and imagine that they are only what they know about themselves . . . Rationalism and doctrinairism are the disease of our time; they pretend to have all the answers . . . the mythic side of man is given short shrift nowadays [for] scientific man cannot permit [the mythic].[9]

> Reason sets the boundaries far too narrowly for us . . . The more critical reason dominates, the more impoverished life becomes .

---

[9] Carl Jung, *Memories, Dreams, Reflections,* 1961, 1962, 1962, Vintage Books Edition, April, 1989, p. 300.

. . Overvalued reason has this in common with political absolutism; under its dominion the individual is pauperized.[10]

And in Francine's folder, a quote attributed to Albert Einstein, "The intuitive mind is a sacred gift and the rational mind is a faithful servant. We have created a society that honors the servant and has forgotten the gift."

"Hmmm, a pauperized individual, which is?" Justin seemed intrigued, while Sherry responded, "Psychologically impoverished. When abstractions of the mind in doctrines or the abstraction of numbers in science are over-valued, regarded exclusively, one's unique nature fades into being a member of a creed, a statistic, a role to fit into. Living a half-brained life. One's full potential is not brought forth, realized, living a half-brained awareness, the essence of a person becomes obscured. Instead, there is stunted, inadequate affirmation of one's total reality—dissatisfaction, boredom, chasing shallow novelty, superficial emptiness which contributes to addiction, compulsion, and other maladies and hollow eccentricities."

"Whole-brain functioning people will save the world?" Justin suggested in jest. "Maybe," Sherry agreed, as she retrieved another piece of paper printed from the internet, in Francine's folder, "Northwestern University now offers whole-brain engineering. Here, straight from its website."

At Northwestern Engineering, we do more than educate great engineers. We empower our students to become whole-brain engineers. This means integrating the elements of left-brain thinking—analysis, logic, synthesis, and math—with the kind of right-brain thinking that fosters intuition, metaphorical thought, and creative problem solving. To lead effectively, you must master both.

There was yet another scrap of paper in Francine's folder, "Contemplative Neuroscience Studies at Harvard and elsewhere—sometimes joined with Integrative Medicine."

---

[10] Carl Jung, *Memories, Dreams, Reflections,* p. 302.

Justin was impressed, "Francine does keep up with things, doesn't she. When she and mom first met, with Francine new in this country buying her high rise, she seemed like an aunt to me, or at least a relative as the two of them spoke French and bonded. Since I didn't have aunts in this country, I guessed an aunt must be someone like Francine—a smart aunt."

Sherry complimented, "I can't imagine myself having a better mentor." And then, as if wrapping-up their long discussion on brain-hemispheres, she added, "To get a quick look at what McGilchrist understands about the competing brain hemispheres, see the short, animated video: *The Divided Brain* on YouTube."

Sherry momentarily backtracked, "Speaking of a smart aunt reminds me of something similar in healing the personality. The Swiss psychiatrist Carl Jung found generational-ancestral healing too little dealt with in psychotherapy, though in his own life he found such important, as if things or question were left unanswered or incompletely answered by parents, grandparents, and more distant ancestors, waiting for his answers. I therefore appreciate the Catholic idea of praying for those who have died, and also that I might be open to insights about healings needed in my own ancestry, even if I don't yet know specifics of those needed healings."

As if Justin didn't want more talk of ancestry, he asked what was in the colorful small box on the table. Sherry opened the box which held Francine's mobius band, "Imprinted with *yin-yang* traits, which might be called brain-hemisphere traits, or traditional masculine-feminine characteristics" She put the band on her wrist, moving it to show how words alternately appear and disappear.

She clarified, "*Traditional, culturally-conditioned* masculine-feminine isn't the same as *innate* masculine-feminine, but can we pull them apart?" Justin gently moved her hand closer to the hurricane lamp on the table so as to better see the words on the mobius band. He held her hand as he moved the band and then stopped the movement, "I guess tonight we've mostly talked about a mobius band that doesn't move—being stuck in a mindset that evaluates itself as knowing more than it does, which the left-hemisphere apparently tends to do."

Sherry and Justin were enthralled in the tender touch of their hands, or so it seemed to Sherry. The same was true a bit later in the all-encompassing, incomparable, lengthy, pleasurable hug they shared, despite masks, as they said goodnight. Was Sherry correct that romance existed between herself and Justin?

CHAPTER ELEVEN

An Ounce of Prevention

As the Covid crisis continued, Cynthia realized with Lucky and Totem gone, she wanted a puppy, though she hadn't yet mentioned this to anyone. She didn't know whether she wanted Sherry to accompany her to an animal shelter, or whether she wanted no one influencing her choice of the pet.

Cynthia knew the ins and outs of training a puppy, and the vigilance she'd need to keep a puppy from disrupting the Kendrick household which was full of adult activity, with Charles's bedroom her father's working from home office, Dee's continued use of the guest bedroom as her library and work space, and Cynthia in her old bedroom room now bursting with accumulations of her college years spilling over into the garage, until the day when she would eventually have her own apartment. A puppy would be a headache yet Cynthia wanted one.

She wanted a cuddly, amusing companion. It was somewhat embarrassing to admit to herself that nephew Monty might have filled her "want" had she gotten the job in the Kansas City area, where she could have seen him frequently. She didn't regard her want a maternal drive, but rather, a yearning for childlike companionship; having one's own special bond with fierce loyalty and affection between herself and the dog. She wanted that satisfaction, free of the complications she'd found so far in human romance.

She didn't expect a romantic possibility during the pandemic, living in Sandshell. If university life hadn't resulted in a lasting relationship, Sandshell was unlikely to provide such. There was a chance she would never marry, she realized, which wasn't altogether distressing, for she knew better than to be overly concerned, fortified by the fact that women have choices in today's world.

She'd recently watched a romantic drama on TV, where the female protagonist made unfortunate choices looking for romance, and suffered painful consequences. And then Cynthia knew why Benjamin Franklin's words, "An ounce of prevention is worth a pound of cure," had come to her.

The words came at the end of sleep next morning after watching the movie the evening before, wherein she felt annoyed with the stupidity of the female in the movie, and then became critical of her own judgmental reaction to the character in the movie.

In summary, if the protagonist in the movie had had an ounce of insight about herself and romance, she could have saved herself a lot of pain. Benjamin Franklin's words fit what was going on inside Cynthia at the time of the dream.

Cynthia concluded that sleep brought Franklin's words which provided perspective to her jumbled feelings about romance. But what mechanism inside her produced this profound statement? God, or the Holy Spirit? Innate wisdom? which may be the same as God or Holy Spirit. Cynthia was pleased with the prospect that guiding wisdom might be alive within her, in her dreams.

She talked with Dee about this, who understood and affirmed Cynthia's conclusion, adding, "If you want a non-religious term, you can call it synchronicity. However, what is synchronicity?" "And what's the Holy Spirit?" Cynthia asked.

To Cynthia's question, Dee replied with a quip, "The Holy Spirit is one-third of the Trinity." Then, more seriously, "There's the "Father" in Christianity, which to me is primary Being, Being Itself, Timeless Beingness, (God). Then, along came Jewish Jesus, the "Son" part of the Trinity, who knew how to relate fully to Being in contrast to countless humans over eons who, in varying degrees, lost vital connection to Essential Essence (God, the Father-Spirit).

"Jewish Jesus was killed by crucifixion, a common execution of his day, for disturbing his culture's status quo through his obvious intact God-connection. And then, Jesus' followers simultaneously knew he'd died yet experienced he was alive, and came to know when he permanently left the earthly realm, he'd opened a path to Eternal Spirit, Holy Spirit, the Divine Father-God, Total Being, available to all who want IT.

"The Holy Spirit is the third part of the Trinity, and this is my version of the Trinity, which likely has something wrong with it, as various explanations of the Trinity have been declared heretical."

Cynthia quietly listened, and then summarized, "So, Being Itself is the fabric of the universe?" Dee replied, "I'd say so." Cynthia asked further, "And the label 'Father' is a metaphor?" Dee nodded in agreement, adding, "Most people don't recognize God as father is a metaphor." Cynthia inquired, "What do you mean?"

Dee explained, "With 'Father' as unrecognized metaphor, Being Itself becomes viewed as a masculine God. Specialists in religion, such as theologians, may acknowledge Being Itself as Spirit without gender, but in everyday terms, God becomes considered masculine." This is another gender issue in today's culture, Dee silently realized again.

Benjamin Franklin's advice, "An ounce of prevention is worth a pound of cure," remained important to Cynthia. Not only his saying, but its spontaneous arrival with no effort on her part, left its impact on her, and was to become even more relevant.

CHAPTER TWELVE

Puppies

Cynthia's desire for a puppy was greeted with enthusiasm by Dee and Zach. Cynthia liked the name Pickett for the new pet, which means she would pick-it, choose it herself, alone, no one going to the animal shelter with her. She purposely did not go to animal shelter websites to see pictures. She wanted no pre-conceived notions—only raw spontaneity between herself and the puppy who would become hers. She was excited.

One morning, mid-morning, she was wearing a face mask, waiting in the sun in line at an animal shelter, observing Covid pandemic protocol. She'd underestimated the process, how hot it would be waiting in line, and in her excitement left her water in the car, which she seriously regretted, as she grew more miserable. There were more people than she'd counted on. The line was longer than she'd expected. She was annoyed and frustrated with herself leaving her water in the car.

Then, she declared to herself, "Why suffer today when I can return tomorrow, earlier when it will be cooler, remember to bring the water with me—and a shade umbrella." She left the waiting line.

In the parking lot, as she opened the car door, a male voice nearby asked, "How long did it take for you to get inside the shelter?" To which she answered, "I didn't go in—got too hot standing in line, forgot my water, I'll be back another day. If you don't have water, you'll need some."

He replied, "I'll be fine." She insisted, "Believe me, you'll need water" as she walked, face mask on, toward the hood of his car, placing there a bottle of water, having noticed a sticker on his car rear window THE MERRIWEATHER SCHOOL. "I'll be teaching second grade at the Merriweather School this Fall," while noticing the sandy-colored short hair and ruddy complexion of this average height guy.

He, putting on his face mask, "I teach biology grades 9-12 there. It's a great school. I've completed three years. I'm Quinn Collins."

"I'm Cynthia Kendrick. I've met other Merriweather teachers online, but you are the first live specimen other than personnel who hired me. I don't want to be teaching online. This isn't how I expected to begin my career."

"It's not ideal for the most part," he agreed, "but it's doable."

She requested, "I wish you'd let me know how things here at the shelter work out for you," as she handed him a business card, which she'd had a batch made to celebrate her hiring."

That evening, Quinn texted and sent a photo of Bios, his mostly brown, large, short-hair dog, mixed breed, a youngish female brought to the shelter when her family could no longer deal with working from home while having children at home all day every day because of Covid.

Quinn had plans, "I expect Bios and I will become running mates. I do marathons and my dog Fella who died a few months ago was my faithful running companion. I expect the same from Bios." Cynthia guessed, "The name Bios is connected to biology?"

"Yes, Bios means life in Greek. BIOS is also an acronym for Basic Input/Output System in computer language. I expect Bios to be very savvy electronically, a "with it" companion in every way. Haven't yet told her my expectations."

Cynthia asked questions about the pet adoption process, as she intended to return early tomorrow morning to be near the front of the line with water and an umbrella. Quinn's input was helpful the next morning when Cynthia adopted a brown, toy, female Pekingese, immediately named Pickett.

Pickett had been brought to the shelter at the end of shelter hours yesterday. She wasn't at the shelter when Cynthia was there yesterday morning—a stroke of good fortune that Cynthia left her water in the car yesterday, and thus didn't pursue the adoption process yesterday!

Cynthia learned Pickett had been named Pixie by a female senior citizen in her eighties who found caring for a pet at her age was increasingly not manageable. Cynthis liked the name Pixie-Pickett for this year-old darling Cynthia could scarcely wait to introduce to dad-Zach and mum-Dee. Pixie-Pickett had a name bigger than her little body. Now, everyone in the household but Cynthia had a hyphenated name. Pixie-Pickett reminded them of Dee's long-ago pet, Mister.

That same day, Cynthia texted Quinn and sent photos of Pixie-Pickett. And thus, they texted and sent photos back and forth regularly until deciding to meet at a park with their pets, but not before Cynthia was certain Quinn was not married or engaged to be married, after the Pablo debacle.

At the park, petite Pixie-Pickett was overwhelmed by big Bios and the tiny Pekingese demanded, with tiny paws pleadingly planted up on Cynthia's leg while whining, wanting to be held by Cynthia so as to not be pummeled by Bios. Finally, the little dog's piercing bark intimidated the big dog and kept Bios at bay. The canines eventually reached compromises on how they would co-exist, interact, even play together.

Conversation was easy between Cynthia and Quinn because of The Merriweather School, for Cynthia learned about students, parents, other teachers, staff and administration. From teachers she was working with online she learned Quinn was regarded an effective teacher, though they didn't know him well personally because they were in the elementary school.

Cynthia learned from Quinn he was from Indiana, the middle child with four siblings, from an intact family. He'd been in the army in Afghanistan, (two all-paid vacations to Afghanistan, he told her), had been in a seminary for a year to become a priest, left seminary for regular college and then a Master's degree in biology, runs marathons, came to Florida on a whim, hoping one day to live on a Greek island.

"Permanently live on a Greek island?" she asked him.

"More like summers on different Greek islands," he explained, "My sister and I went to Athens, Ephesus, the island of Patmos, with a tour group two years ago."

"Why did you leave the seminary?"

"I realized I wasn't cut-out to be a priest though I'm Irish Catholic from before Adam and Eve."

"Remarkably long family history," she said in a tone which revealed she understood how outrageous his comment was. Cynthia felt her life by comparison was staid, boring, living her whole life in Florida, having left the country only once for Scotland and the Orkney Islands with parents and grandparents, which was an exceptional experience. Now with the pandemic, she wasn't even going to Kansas City or Clarksdale. She was stuck in Sandshell.

With their dogs, Cynthia and Quinn continued to meet in the park. Conversation was easy: about their pets, The Merriweather School, the future of Covid, and politics. Cynthia daydreamed of an evening on the Kendrick patio with Quinn and Bios. Fond memories of patio dinners summers ago remained with her.

CHAPTER THIRTEEN

Marriage Troubles

Cynthia took Pixie-Pickett to meet Sherry, though they were unable to be on the balcony because precious petite Pixie-Pickett might be able to squeeze between spaces in the balcony railing, Cynthia feared. The dog sat on Cynthia's lap for awhile on the balcony until both got too hot from the arrangement, and the three moved inside to air-conditioned comfort.

Sherry readily spoke of feeling stressed over the necessity of virtual-therapy these days of Covid. She admitted being overwhelmed with marriage-counseling, realizing having never been married left her dependent on Francine in this area, and she was rather consumed by her inadequacy.

Francine, with the permission of a married couple had taken to video-taping virtual sessions with the couple, sometimes together, sometimes singly. They consented to Francine sharing their taped sessions with Sherry.

Overall, Sherry was grateful for Francine's ongoing detailed teaching. Just now, Francine was sharing step-by-step with Sherry, therapy session videos, with the consent of clients Kelly and Paul, married six years, in their mid- thirties, parents of four-year-old son, Connor.

Kelly had grown-up in a rough-and-tumble, large, Irish-background family in the Boston MA area. Paul was from Vancouver, Canada. The two met online, both had the desire to live in a warm climate, and chose Florida. He was in computers. She was taking college classes.

Paul began the first counseling session saying his agenda was for Kelly to be "truthful" about her behavior, especially her recent outrageous telephone call. Kelly said the real truth was that if he hadn't taken Connor to Vancouver, she would never have had to get so angry, and Connor probably wouldn't have gotten sick, delaying their return to Florida. Paul was not derailed. "I want you to know how angry I am at your cursing and swearing at me just because I invited you to Vancouver for a weekend while waiting for Connor to recover from his bronchitis and ear infection, and the three of us would come home together, and you know perfectly well Connor, on occasion, has gotten ill here at home." With a look of shocked horror on her face, Kelly started to cry and talk, "What was so wrong with what I said on the telephone? I didn't want to go to Vancouver. I hate flying."

Paul was confidently primed, "My parents are my parents and they are going to continue living in Vancouver. I am going to Vancouver from time to time to see them and I want Connor to know them. This is not going to change. Are we going to go through this every time?"

Kelly was crying harder now and uncharacteristically meek. She said, "Why are you being so mean? I thought with a therapist present you would be more civil."

Paul did not hold back. "I wanted a therapist present to help keep us on track. I want you to know that since your latest swearing fest, I have been seriously considering divorce, not for that one incident but because I find living with you difficult because of your emotional outbursts. I don't want a lifetime of that. I am no longer willing to live with all of the emotional stuff and I don't want Connor growing up with it."

Kelly's crying first increased and then turned into stunned staring. Finally she said, "I have always thought you would divorce me, just like your parents divorced." Yes, Kelly had expressed this fear to Paul before. Paul was patient. "I am not mentioning divorce to threaten you."

Kelly began a fog of emotional combat. "Why talk when you've already made up your mind, right?" She looked at Francine, seeking confirmation.

Paul continued, "I don't mention divorce to be mean. I just want you to know that I am not afraid of the option now. I simply realize turmoil doesn't have to be part of daily living."

Kelly was livid, "Being around your sanctimonious stubborn father taught you how to live, no doubt," she acidly spewed, "and his quiet, tranquil household was so satisfactory that his wife, your mother, ran off with the friend of a friend."

Paul struggled to not respond to her scrappy words, "Kelly, I just want you to know that I want and need more peace in our relationship and less anger."

Kelly was ready with a barrage. "And what you want and need must be what is right? What about my wants and needs? The coldness you've shown since you've been home tells me that my wants and needs don't matter. First it was jetlag and then all the work at the office. Well, I don't know how long jetlag lasts for you and how high the stacks of work must be piled at the office, but your remoteness, your lack of interest in me is emotional bullying, I can tell you that."

Paul kept calm with great difficulty. "The truth is that I am unable to be physically and emotionally close to you when I feel estranged from you. I want things to be better."

Kelly started moderately angry and escalated. "And I'm the one who has to change, right? I have to change my basic personality so that you can have more peace and tranquility. Does that make any sense? Who the hell wouldn't like that; get the other person to change; blame the other person for everything, and do it with the threat of divorce? Don't tell me you're not a street-fighter, which you sometimes accuse me of. You just fight in a more orderly way than I do, but you're fighting right now for what you want and you're doing it pretty dirty, too, by threatening me with divorce."

Paul was not stumped. "I'm not threatening you with divorce. I just want you to know I'm not afraid of divorce if it has to come to that."

Kelly was crying hard now.

CHAPTER FOURTEEN

Verbal Combat

Paul continued calmly, "What I most hope for us is that we can have a good marriage and make a good home for Connor. What I least want is a divorce. However, I will not settle for a life of continuing conflict, searing emotions, rage that's ready to erupt at any moment. I don't want Connor to grow up with that either."

Kelly shot back, "Do you think I want Connor to grow up with what you just described? I also don't want Connor growing up with laziness and I see how you'd rather lie on the couch with an electronic device and entertain yourself, with video games, and who knows what else, for hours on end, sometimes laughing out loud. It's as if neither Connor nor I exist. I want you to be more of my life; in my life. I don't want Connor growing up with your stubbornness, and I think you can be so damn obstinate it hurts. I want you to change just like you want me to change."

Kelly continued, "I know a lot about my flaws, probably more than you know about yours. One night while you were gone, I went through hell, but I haven't even had a chance to tell you about that. It's one of the most important things that has ever happened to me and several times I've tried to tell you about it, but you'd always bring up something about what you had to do with Connor when he was sick in Vancouver, or stories about Connor when he was playing with his cousins, or you'd bring up a detail about work at the office since you're back. You clearly don't want to hear about me."

Paul admitted, "You're right. I came home with an agenda. I want you to apologize for the way you talked to me on the telephone when you said you weren't coming to Vancouver. I have been wanting, and still want you to apologize for all the times your emotions, particularly anger, have created so much trouble in our marriage. I want you to admit that you are an active volcano waiting to erupt. I want you to stop diagnosing everybody else and use a few labels on yourself. I have a lot of anger towards you and I don't think it's going to go away unless we get it out in the open."

Kelly pouted calmly, "Once again you've put your agenda forth, but you haven't begun to hear from me. I just told you about something especially important that happened to me when I was here alone. You haven't asked anything about when I was here by myself. Let's be sure it's out in the open that your agenda is obviously more important than my needs.

She continued, "Sometimes I feel you're like a young boy who has to be doted-on, paid attention to, encouraged, needing to get his own way. I see a selfish side of you that you are quite blind to. It's your way or no way. Just like I have to change or there will be a divorce. But I want you to realize I learned a lot about myself through hours of hell when I was here by myself."

Paul cut her short, "I went through my own hell in Vancouver because of your tongue lashing. I try to forget about it, but it won't go away. For me it shows what is wrong in this relationship."

Kelly immediately responded. "Why are you so negative when I admit I have faults."

Paul interrupted, "Like your vicious talk? Swearing, cursing at me ..."

Kelly countered, "OK, I am overly sensitive. Do you know how much it hurts for me to admit this to you? I went through hours of hellish torment here by myself. I am sorry for whatever pain I caused you but maybe I had to create the mess I did so I could meet my demons. I'm sorry for what you went through, but I learned so much."

Paul's anger burst forth, "Is this as honest as you can get? *You* got to meet *your* demons and *you* learned so much. Obviously, *you* are incapable of getting-over *yourself*. I am sick and tired of the wrangling. Marriage should be easier than this." But theirs wasn't and obviously his parents' marriage wasn't either. Paul ended, "We both have a lot to learn."

His last words agitated Kelly who shrieked, "I have just spilled my guts and that's all you have to say, 'We both have a lot to learn.' Connor could have done better than that." She was weeping.

Paul was bewildered: he should let her write the script and he could read it on cue. If he doesn't say what she wants, this evening isn't going to work; their marriage won't work. She is impossible and their marriage is impossible, Paul concluded mentally.

Kelly continued, "I want you to accept my apology. I poured myself out and you came back with the piss-ant reply, '*We* both have a lot to learn.' Well, *my* apology several times included the words *I am sorry* which you apparently did not hear."

Paul answered back, "I heard you say *I'm sorry* twice and the first time you ended the sentence with how the situation helped *you* meet *your* demons and the second *I'm sorry* ended with how much *you* had learned. It seemed to me it was all about *you* again."

Kelly agreed, "*My* apology was about *me* and what *I* had done. How else could an apology be?"

Paul answered, "I can only say hooking your gains onto my losses seems self-serving to me."

She asked, "What the hell does that mean?"

Paul explained. "Twice you said *I'm sorry* and each time added what *you* learned and I'm saying what you learned is irrelevant in the apology. Though it may be true that you learned some lessons, they shouldn't be part of your apology."

"Where did you learn such hair-splitting horseshit?" Kelly flung at him. Kelly regularly told him his logical approach was maddening and only made things worse. She often claimed he sounded like a damn philosopher who didn't know what he's talking about.

Paul wanted to pull his hair out. No, with strange humor he told himself, he'd rather pull her hair out. This was typical Kelly, who has as much a chance learning to be more logical as he has understanding her illogical maneuverings. He has to admit her scattered, all-over-the-place approach works for her. She is a scrappy fighter.

Right then, she skillfully threw Paul's word *irrelevant* back at him. "If you want to talk *irrelevant*, that's what your rubbish comment, 'We both have a lot to learn,' is to me." Despite her mocking, Paul kept his cool and defended his statement, "I feel my words are a generous acknowledgment that neither of us is perfect." Kelly countered, "My apology isn't about you or your generous observations."

It was a stalemate. Paul felt their relationship was a perpetual stalemate. Whatever "truth" Paul had naively felt might work, couldn't happen with Kelly. She was not a systematic thinker, and maybe he was an underdeveloped feeler.

Kelly looked at Francine and asked pointedly, "What do you think?"

Clarity had surfaced in Francine's mind as the two-track conversation of Kelly and Paul unfolded. Francine said to Kelly, "What words do you want to hear from Paul?" Kelly replied, "I want him to say he accepts my apology about hurting him and that he forgives me."

Then Francine asked Paul what words he wanted from Kelly and he said, "I want her to admit that she was outrageously mean on the telephone and that she often says things that are insane, stupid, irrational, preposterous, and that she will stop such absurd, crazy behavior."

Kelly summarized, "You want me to confess to being a nut case, and to promise I'll stop being a nut case."

Paul did not disagree with her summary. He added, "I want you to admit your behavior is often not normal."

She re-phrased her situation, "I admit I may sometimes be overly emotional, and I want desperately for you to forgive me."

To Paul it seemed she was more interested in his forgiving than in her admitting her destructive behaviors, but he said simply, "I guess I can try to forgive you."

Kelly was not yet finished. "To forgive me for what?"

She was merciless, Paul thought: another power play, controller to the end. Or maybe she wanted to drink the poison of her own making. He'd seen her be merciless with herself. Or was she compiling a tally sheet to use later? After all, Kelly was a scrapper.

This time Paul uncharacteristically wanted to pin her to the wall. Too often he'd let her get by with outrageous behavior; kept himself from saying all he wanted to say. Not now. He was more forthright than he'd ever been with words meant to sting, he said: "I suppose it would be good if I could forgive you for the cruel things you said recently on the telephone, and your gazillion overreactions to almost everything most of the time." He made the sweeping statement he'd been wanting to make for quite some time.

Unusual for Kelly, she was levelheaded, even jovial: "Well, you got another jab in but at least we are not headed for divorce court tonight. Am I right?"

"Correct, but we don't know about tomorrow," he responded with a serious tone. Kelly winced slightly but did not answer back.

CHAPTER FIFTEEN

Virtual Online Therapy

Francine shared in depth with Sherry the marital difficulty of clients Kelly and Paul. Francine felt their problems were not about either one being particularly mentally unhealthy, but rather, the two of them were drastically different psychological "types," which they did already know.

Kelly and Paul continued to bring their troubled relationship to therapy, sometimes separately, sometimes together. Paul was convinced their core problem was he is a thinking-type person, whereas Kelly is "all-feelings." To him, Kelly's judgments, interpretations, conclusions, seemed hotheaded and out-of-kilter. If only she could be more rational, more careful processing facts. She sometimes acted as if being emphatic was enough to make something factual. And he often ignored her observations and opinions because it was exhausting to constantly dispute or question her so-called "reasonings." Kelly hated being ignored.

Paul, in an individual zoom session with Francine, voiced bitter annoyance with Kelly using diagnostic labels she'd learned in psychology classes in college, not sure she understood them correctly herself. "She uses the labels as weapons; thus having some kind of power over others."

Paul concluded he realized he shouldn't have married Kelly, but then, Connor wouldn't exist. Paul wondered if he'd known Kelly better before they married, if they hadn't lived together so quickly; if he hadn't moved into *her* apartment; been dependent on *her* while he looked for a job and became acclimated to his life in the U.S. Yes, there were always bumps in their relationship, but her recent behavior was simply too much, though he'd often received the sting of her sharp-edged tongue. She was a very sensitive person; however, her sensitivity didn't extend to others. He didn't understand whether, "when she is angry, she chooses to be as mean as she can be, or whether she isn't aware of how callous and mean she is."

The truth was, Paul confessed to Francine, he wanted to leave Kelly more than once before they married. He thought of returning to Vancouver, but didn't want to face family and friends in Vancouver, plus he liked the freedom to pursue opportunities in the United States. And in ways, he was attracted to Kelly, perhaps because they were opposite personality types.

Paul confided in Francine the thoughts that poured into his head as he had sat in the quiet of a Catholic church in Boston, where he was living with Kelly before they were married, and after a rousing spat, when if he'd had any sense, he'd gone back to Canada. However, that day, he'd walked out of the apartment, found the church, and walked-into the quiet to think.

Paul was no longer in the habit of praying, though he had gone to Catholic school and memorized prayers. He now considered praying a superstitious reflex which occurs when people are frightened. Religion has a lot to do with superstition, ignorance, and human fear, Paul told Francine. Paul's regard for science caused him to view the Church's attempts to quash Galileo as arrogance and ignorance. In his early schooling and religious education, he had felt manipulated to think along certain dogmatic lines. He had great resistance to this and easily shared his father's negative reaction against the "authority" of the church, though his father had been raised Catholic.

Paul concluded in Francine's office that he himself was more Catholic than anything else, but religion for the most part is a crutch for the masses and a self-perpetuating institution for the benefit of hierarchy and other clergy. He said, "I remember in the Boston church that day agreeing with Karl Marx that religion is the opiate of the people." And then he was quiet. Francine did not comment but waited for him to continue.

"Yet, I agreed that Connor be baptized, as a part of family tradition, and because that's what Kelly wanted." Paul was quiet again. Then, he said, "In the Boston church that day I felt tears welling in my eyes, and to distract myself, began looking at the ornate, high-rising, splendid architecture. I wondered: what made people go to the expense and effort of building such a church?

"Well, people do a lot of things, many of them stupid. And I told myself I was stupid, too, for marrying Kelly after meeting her through a chat room on the internet. Then, with emotions beginning to overwhelm, I again distracted myself, looking at vigil candles burning at a side altar, and noticed the church smelled like a church, saturated with the scent of burning candles and incense from countless Masses.

"I wondered to myself, 'How many baptisms, marriages and funerals had taken place here? It is strange that people need ceremonies, rituals, places of worship. People in the past were often uneducated and needed something, someplace to go to help them get through life. The priests had more education than the general populace, so the priests were oracles on religious and practical matters like legal documents which the poor and uneducated could not understand on their own.'"

These were the thoughts he shared with Francine before returning to the topic of Kelly, who was raised Catholic and described herself as spiritual-not-religious. Paul wondered aloud, "If her spirituality works so well for her, why doesn't it help her control her anger, help her not be so critical of others, moderate her foul language, which she knows I find disagreeable, and help her be more patient with her family, my family, and people in general?"

Questions about the future engulfed him: should he divorce Kelly? Then there would be a custody battle. Paul's voice choked as he shared with Francine the swirling storm in his feelings, his thoughts.

Francine and Kelly had an individual zoom session when Kelly was in a desperate state. She spoke of "the friggin' pile of crap" in her life, her marriage. She wished Paul knew the pain "his jackass stubbornness" caused. Kelly was prone to migraines and her head was beginning to ache; she could feel "the g.d. symptoms," though she'd taken medicine. "Life is one big f-ing mess," Kelly reaffirmed, beginning to cry. She was in "a very bad place." She was blaming, agitated, irritated, angry about her childhood, her siblings, her marriage, her whole life.

She screeched, "My God! How could one grow up sane in a house with an alcoholic father and a mother who blamed 'drink' for everything, blamed him for everything, never her own shortcomings. And who wouldn't drink married to my mother's half-baked personality. I wanted to go to college and someday have a decent marriage. No one helped me find my way into college, and a decent marriage hasn't happened so far. I always tried to do thoughtful things for my siblings and friends, but people are such pigs, taking and using whoever and whatever they can. No wonder the world is such a mess. People are users with no awareness, and want to remain clueless," Kelly fumed.

"On my own, I've earned a degree in psychology. I think Paul resents what I know about psychology. He doesn't want to look at himself and what he needs to change, though, as you see when we have a session together, he knows plenty about what I need to change in myself. I believe he knows he needs God, religion, spirituality, but doesn't take a step in that direction for himself while belittling my own prayer practices. I do sometimes light candles at home and spend quiet time.

"He's convinced I'm too much a 'feeler.' I tell him he needs to get in touch with his feelings and maybe he wouldn't have the stomach problems he has. Recently, he has started saying about my migraines, maybe if I could 'think' more clearly, I wouldn't have migraines. I don't believe he even believes that, but is merely mimicking what I say about him."

Francine asked Kelly a hypothetical: "Though divorce would be painful, might being away from Paul be an improvement in your life?" Kelly was slow to answer, "Well, there would always be contact between us because of Connor. I wouldn't want Paul to find someone else, build a family with someone else. I actually don't want him gone, but just want to live with a better version of him," she laughed. Both Kelly and Paul could laugh at their situation, when she wasn't snarling at him and he wasn't ignoring her.

Sherry wondered if she would ever be able to handle this kind of relationship complexity with the insight and poise of Francine. She was being painfully stretched, painfully pulled into the entanglements of what marriage involves. Despite knowing how fortunate she was to be under

Francine's tutelage, despite sometimes wishing she lived in a bigger city though living at the beach at Sandshell, despite having Cynthia, Dee and Zach in Sandshell which made her feel at home, there were pockets of disquiet inside Sherry.

CHAPTER SIXTEEN

Legacy of the 1960s

On a happier note, Cynthia's daydream became reality when Quinn and Bios joined the Kendricks and Pixie-Pickett on the patio for a relaxed evening meal, where strategic social distancing was observed at the long table. Bios and Pixie-Pickett ran together a short while in the backyard before making clear their desire to be in the patio with humans—who were enjoying grilled seafood and fresh vegetables from the garden. The large overhead fan kept everyone physically comfortable, while iced tea, beer, wine, frozen lemon dessert, brought delightful ambience.

The logistics of the meal went smoothly, and so did conversation about the current political divide in the country, which was thought to go back to the 1960s, a time of drastic change.

Cynthia and Quinn read about these years in history books, while Dee and Zach lived through the 60s. At the time, the war in Vietnam and the military draft which fed the war seemed increasingly pointless and destructive which spawned protests against, and loss of confidence in, governmental policies, the government as an institution, as well as other traditional institutions including corporations, colleges and universities, and institutional religion.

There was growing awareness of racial and gender inequalities and implications of a generation gap. The flower children spoke of feeling alienated. They wanted change. They wanted to know who they were as individuals. They wanted to blast open society to new ways of being. They wanted peace in Vietnam and in themselves. They wanted to live in harmony with others and formed communes. The label "flower children" came from the lyrics of the song "San Francisco," "If you're going to San Francisco, be sure to wear some flowers in your hair," which inspired some to wear flowers and pass them out to passersby. Though the hippie movement began in this country the ideas spread around the world.

Who were the Flower Children? Also called Hippies and Beatniks, they were a substantial subculture searching for spirituality beginning in the early 1960s and declining by the mid-70s. Some concluded that if this subculture was what spirituality was about, who needs it. Others saw the flower children as a breath of fresh air in a toxic cultural climate at a turbulent time. Others saw them as an out-of-control challenge to a status quo that needed to be challenged; if only it had happened in a better, wiser way.

The Flower Children were symptomatic of something. The word symptom has the same root as the word symbol. Had this been understood, implementing the symbol might have been done with greater wisdom. This was not the case. Something was coming forth, but what?

The birth control pill was approved by the FDA in 1960, which encouraged sexual freedom. The Human Potential Movement emerged. Esalen in Big Sur, CA became a mecca for exploring the frontiers of the human personality. There was optimistic expectation that societies improve as individuals develop their full potential; that the world gets better one person at a time. The astrological Age of Aquarius was expected to usher in a New Age of love, peace, harmony. An open-ended pluralistic attitude developed about religions, cultures, individual choices. New Age religion appeared.

The Flower Children wanted qualitative change in themselves and culture. They searched in T-groups, sensitivity groups, Gestalt groups, marathons (nude and otherwise), Transcendental Meditation groups, Primal Scream groups. They were looking for a shift from self-alienation to self-actualization, a term from the work of psychologist Abraham Maslow (1908-1970).

Dee pointed out, "Maslow's hierarchy of needs, first articulated in 1943, has parallels with fourfold exegesis, which I am using with Jesus' parables. There is nothing new under the sun."

The patio group continued constructing their view of the flower children who epitomized a return to childlikeness. Their yearning for spirituality, harmony, peace, was being sought in a culture described as becoming a "military industrial complex," by President Eisenhower when he left office in 1961. The flower children were reacting against unquestioned approaches to living life. However, not knowing how to facilitate what they sought, they heightened awareness with hallucinogenic and other drugs, sex, and various means of achieving altered states of consciousness. They used psychedelic artifacts, music, drugs, light shows, colors, art work, to intensify the personality. They wanted to experience themselves; their own subjectivity after overvalued objectivity in science.

They searched for spiritual gurus and meditative practices, especially from India and other Asian cultures. The Beatles' "All You Need Is Love," was a flagship song of the day. They touted universal love; threw away their timepieces so as to live in the moment. Culture needed to change; look at the mess society was in; look where the old values had taken culture.

The war in Vietnam was finally over in 1975. The New Age movement began to decline though its legacy is still with us. And what is that legacy? Some say illicit drugs, sexual irresponsibility, eroding traditional values. While this might be a legitimate critique, their legacy embodies more: more legal clout to back up respect for the civil rights of everyone; more awareness of the need to respect the earth and creation; more regard for diversity and differences in religions, cultures, individuals and their choices; new genres in music and the arts in general; organic foods, homeopathic medicines; recognition of becoming a global community.

Other important events of the 1960s took place alongside the flower children's experiments in living. The Charismatic Movement began in different Christian denominations in the 1960s. Split-brain research took place. The Second Vatican Council, 1962-65 was underway, followed by the 1965 mutual withdrawals of excommunication edicts between Pope and Patriarch.

The 1960s and 70s brought change. How might the flower children have left a better legacy? If only they'd had more discernment. They had little discernment. They lacked sound judgment; the ability to make healthy choices. They were, for the most part quite young.

The flower children used both drugs and gurus to search for spiritually. They mixed universal love, human love, and genital pleasure. They con-fused liberating freedom with hedonistic excess.

Though some became "Jesus Freaks" and some liked St. Francis of Assisi, the flower children did not typically turn to organized Christianity in their spiritual search. And this is revealing. They wanted the experiential spirituality of Asian religions, not instruction and explanation which too often is what it seemed Christianity provided. They seemed not to know about the Christian mystical, contemplative tradition. How could this be?

By now on the Kendrick patio, Bios and Pixie-Pickett had been asleep on the concrete floor for some time. The hour was late. The patio group concluded that today's toxic politics are echoes rooted, at least partially, to changes in brain-hemisphere preferences dating back to the 60s—new ways of seeing and approaching life and living.

The Kendrick patio evening had been an oasis in the Covid-stay-at-home desert, which adjourned with utterances that the participants would convene again.

CHAPTER SEVENTEEN

Looking Elsewhere

Next day, Quinn was still wondering why the '60s didn't, for the most part, see young people scrambling to Christianity to find answers to their spiritual questions. Why did they look elsewhere? With Vatican II beginning at that time, what did it have to say about the contemplative tradition in the church?

Quinn was looking in his book containing the sixteen documents which came out of Vatican II, held in Rome, which was spread over four years in the autumn months of 1962, 63, 64, 65 with much work done in-between by various commissions. The first session was attended by 2,450 churchmen out of 2,908 entitled to attend. Some bishops were too old or infirm to attend, and some bishops in Communist countries were not allowed to travel. Thirty-five observers from other Christian churches attended the first session and their numbers increased in following sessions.

Quinn was searching for something specific in the Vatican documents book. He found one index entry on *contemplative life*, mentioned in the *Decree on The Church's Missionary Activity*, which states traditions of asceticism and contemplation sown by God in certain ancient cultures before the preaching of the gospel be incorporated into the Christian religious life, adapted to local conditions. The last sentence in the section reads, 'The contemplative life should be restored everywhere, because it belongs to the fullness of the church's presence.'

Quinn wondered whether "everywhere" meant the church's presence throughout a specific mission locale, or throughout the church at large? He pondered if the church shouldn't be more about serving the contemplative impulse in humanity rather than the contemplative life belonging to the fullness of the church's presence. Perhaps the contemplative life was different from Quinn's understanding of the words, contemplative prayer, contemplative practice, contemplation.

He tried to make sense of the convergence of '60s flower children, split-brain research, Vatican II, and the Charismatic Renewal which he knew were all taking place at the time. These were monumental events rippling down to today. At the moment, he wished he'd studied history instead of biology, though biology did bring him to know about basic differences between the brain-hemispheres, which did seem close to Dee's heart, and Quinn was fond of Dee and her interests.

The day after the patio dinner, Cynthia realized again the impact on her of Dee's pursuits in religion and split-brain knowledge, including metaphoric discernment with Dee's purple aura cat image. Cynthia wondered what Quinn meant recently when he commented in the park that he'd never had such common interests with any woman he'd been involved with compared to what he and Cynthia shared. What exactly did Quinn mean? Was he saying the two of them were *involved*? Not necessarily. What was his involvement with other women? She didn't know what to make of his statement.

Cynthia felt grudgingly beholden to Dee for having been both mentor and mother-figure. Cynthia's interests which attracted Quinn had basically been absorbed by Cynthia from Dee, which was its own dilemma. In Cynthia's mind, she was unavoidably indebted to Dee.

CHAPTER EIGHTEEN

Worry and Icon

A few days later, Cynthia and Dee, dubbed "Angels of Mercy" by Monique, were routinely delivering vegetables from the Kendrick garden to a homeless shelter, then to Estelle and Francine who needed only small deliveries, living by themselves, and on to Monique's household where Ingrid was caring for grandson "J" while his mother Christiane was at her now re-opened dance studio, and Monique was spending more time on real estate showings. Ingrid prepared the daily meal for James in the wheelchair, as well as doing light housework and tending to "J."

While Dee and Cynthia were delivering fresh vegetables from the garden, Zach was home alone and received a worried phone call from Charles in Clarksdale. The Covid pandemic had Kendal's brother Patrick and wife Brooke moving to Clarksdale where he would work in Montel Furniture and she aspired to teach at the community college sometime in the future.

Because of Covid, high school basketball coach Patrick would no longer be coaching basketball, for the season had been cancelled. He'd only be teaching health and history classes, which did not suit him. Further, Brooke was pregnant and not wanting to teach until the child was a little older.

Charles fretted to his father on the telephone how this might change his position at the furniture store? Could Montel Furniture afford another full-time salary? Charles didn't know the finances of the store. Townspeople would know Patrick as one of their own, while Charles would always be an outsider. There was the ongoing nagging question whether customers would come to favor internet buying over the personal attention they received at Montel Furniture; would the business naturally fade while employees increased? Patrick, having grown up with the store might know the business in ways Charles could never know. Patrick was the son of the owner and boss—Charles would always be the son-in-law. Would Charles and Patrick compete—clash?

Along with these worries, Charles remembered his dad's panic attack years ago over job-related issues. He could never forget that. He didn't want Zach getting stressed, yet he couldn't fully share his concerns with Kendal, for it was her family who owned the furniture store. Charles went to chant in the glass hut more than usual at this time.

Dee and Cynthia would come home to this telephone news. In their absence, Pixie-Pickett was insisting Zach play with her, which was a healthy distraction, while the two food-deliverers were out of the house longer than usual.

For after delivering fresh vegetables out of the garden to a homeless shelter, Dee and Cynthia were at Estelle's door. She insisted they come in so she could show them a recent acquisition, a copy of an icon of Mary, The Virgin of Vladimir also known as Our Lady of Tenderness, in a standing frame so Estelle could move it from place to place in the house. Estelle was glowing with satisfaction as she told them about the icon.

"Please, do you have time for me to talk a bit about the icon. I know you've got a new pet, Cynthia, and this icon is like a new pet to me. She laughed, and began telling about gazing at an icon as practiced in Eastern Christianity, "Gazing epitomizes Eastern Christianity's spirituality. Whereas listening may describe the spirituality of the West, the Eastern tradition became focused on gazing.

"This icon was painted by a Greek at the beginning of the 12th century. However, it has long been in Russia and is considered a Russian icon. Damaged over the centuries; there are hints of alphabet markings in the background. Most of all, for me, the image of tender bonding between humanity and Mary remains intact, which for me is the icon's essence: human-divine relationship. Look at the eyes.

"This is an instance of image over alphabet. What the icon "says" is worth a thousand words, despite whatever words were once on the canvas; the letters are now mostly obliterated, which I suggest may not be important, for language cannot adequately express the experience of gazing at an icon."

Dee and Cynthia were intrigued with what Estelle shared. Cynthia wondered if she would ever be able to get what Estelle found in the icon. Later, she wondered if she gazed at a Mary icon she could finally and fully erase every ounce of her resistance to Dee.

CHAPTER NINETEEN

Psychological Virginity

After visiting Estelle, Cynthia and Dee were off to Francine's to finish their vegetable delivery where they told of Estelle's icon, which ignited topics in Francine. Tele-therapy sessions left Francine hungry for personal contact. Francine invited them to stay for a socially-distanced lunch.

Cynthia telephoned her dad, who said all was fine on the home front. He did not mention Charles's telephone call and job concerns. Zach encouraged they have lunch with Francine, who always provided more than physical food.

Dee and Cynthia shared about Estelle's icon "The Virgin of Vladimir," whereupon the idea of "virgin" became Francine's focus. She showed them the book from which she'd gathered her views on *psychological* virginity, a perspective she found important.

Francine summarized, "My current understanding of "healthy" psychological virginity, whether male or female is that robust psychological virginity is about being "untouched" – pristine (as in a virgin forest or virgin land untouched by human device or contrivance). Such a personality is in touch with its own nature – not unduly impregnated by the collective mindset, group think, fads, mass reactions, but is instead in-touch with its own creative practical wisdom as well as transcendent longing.

"This healthy virginal personality displays an independent mindset, acts with integrity, can cooperate and contribute, is not prone to becoming a doormat. Having been affirmed by being cherished for one's own being, this personality is at home in its own skin, can be content in solitude, is capable of fruitful reflection, recollection, healthy relationships and active engagement.

"Such an adult personality has either somehow found transformation for unhelpful, confounding, inherited, generational, ancestral traits/qualities/tendencies, or is fortunate to have descended from mostly psychologically healthy family trees.

"My current understanding of "damaged" psychological virginity, whether male or female is that wounded psychological virginity is "touchy" – emotionally untouchable, prickly, not-in-touch with oneself, reactionary, peevishly stubborn rather than independent-minded. Out-of-touch with commonsense wisdom, prone to defensive knee-jerk behaviors, impregnated (contaminated) with anger from being psychically (not physically) violated.

"This personality has been run-over roughshod, ravaged by someone else's agenda (perhaps a parent's expectations, neediness, lack of emotional warmth). The damaged personality lacks intrinsic validation, remains unaffirmed, may lack integrity, as if there is a hole in the soul that frightfully, self-consciously, needs admiration to the point of psychologically prostituting one's being, while also stubbornly pushing people away.

This virginally damaged personality's family tree likely includes traits/qualities/tendencies in need of psychological transformation. In my experience, most personalities inherit some generational issues. I have come to wonder whether Mary's immaculate conception (free of original sin) was a way to express the idea she was born into a psychologically healthy, spiritually evolved, a soul—wise family, which was passed on to Jesus. It was a way of explaining extraordinary Jesus."

It was true, lunch with Francine included more than physical food. After delivering vegetables to Monique's house, driving home with Cynthia, Dee knew the Brunch Bunch needed to be brought together through zoom. Estelle's icon gazing and Francine's view on psychological virginity made Dee know the Brunch Bunch needed to share conversation, to be together, even if it would be a zoom session.

Once home, Zach summarized Charles's job worries for Dee and Cynthia, which Pixie-Pickett could not dilute for Zach, despite her puppy antics wanting to be noticed constantly. Charles's fears filled the air in the kitchen as Zach explained Charles's situation. Dee silently recalled Julia's concerns that none of the Montel children followed Marc into the furniture store business. But that was before Kendal and Charles married and moved to Clarksdale. Julia felt guilty about having never been Marc's partner at the store.

Dee was optimistic that Patrick working at the store might additionally relieve Marc's schedule as Charles had done—and relieve Julia's guilt about not working alongside Marc. Charles's job situation could prove negative, positive, or mixed. Waiting without worrying about the Montel Furniture family employee situation was the challenge, Dee realized.

CHAPTER TWENTY

Chagall, Monique's Infatuation

The Brunch Bunch had their first zoom session with Cynthia a known quiet observer in the room with Dee. She had long wanted to know what the four friends talked about when they gathered. That day, each began by telling how she was coping during the pandemic. Monique told how providing Christiane's ex-husband James with a hot meal daily made her not dislike him so much, "I see his incapacities; how grateful we help him. He's not all bad."

Later she elaborated on her new love, the art work of Marc Chagall discovered by her through a real estate client whose house was filled with copies of his paintings. She explained, "I find attraction to these colorful pieces, strange, unusual, not real yet reality in some sense, another reality with flying people, farm animals, a rooster with a blue head, a red donkey or mule. Why his art calls to me is mystery."

Estelle spoke of her fascination with the Mary icon but didn't share grandson Dexter's current difficulties with his parents. She occasionally telephoned him, or he called her. The two of them had a bond, however he found his parents unbearable, and they had the same opinion of him. Dexter's two younger sisters did not seem to have such friction with the parents. Estelle remained concerned about Dexter.

Dee shared the antics of Pixie-Pickett, and expressed her joy of working in the plentiful garden still capable of supplying vegetables for the group. Then, Monique took center-stage, announcing she wanted to say more about Marc Chagall. She was standing at her dining room table, reading from a piece of paper on the open pages of a huge book, "Chagall was born into Hasidic Judaism in Vitebsk, Russia in 1887. He lived various places, but mostly in Paris. He died at the age of 98 in 1985. His paintings reflect the mysticism of Hasidic Judaism, where true reality is hidden behind *things*. His art shows ecstatic movements of the soul never at rest, but dancing, sinking into one's inmost depths," she read from the piece of paper.

Monique put the piece of paper aside and flipped from page to page showing his paintings, while struggling to manage her electronic device and the unwieldy book, and making comments about the many farm animals in the paintings, which to her, depicted sacrifice, meaning humans must sacrifice to care for the animals, who in the end sacrifice their milk, eggs, their strength to pull a wagon and till the earth, and eventually, their very flesh for human food. She showed Chagall's paintings of crucified Christ, which proved her point that a major theme in his work is sacrifice.

Then, trying to open the book to a particular page to read something vital, she knocked her electronic device off the table, which sent her into an excited flurry with peals of laughter, as she clamored to retrieve it and check whether it still worked. Her laughter rippled through the others who were laughing in-synch with Monique, and perhaps also in exaggerated relief of Covid restraints, in the joy of being connected, even remotely, sharing the mishap which wasn't funny, yet it was.

Despite the comic calamity, Monique found what she wanted to read, and explained that though Chagall was Jewish, he painted the crucified Christ. This she explained, "Chagall wrote in a poem to his wife, "Like Christ, I am crucified, fastened to my easel with nails." The friends applauded Monique for her presentation, for her laughter in the mishap, and in relief that her iPad had not been damaged. Monique explained further, "Chagall fulfilled his passion like Christ fulfilled his Passion. Not saying the two were the same, equal in accomplishment or passion."

Then, Estelle said Monique's display of Chagall's art prompted a comment about her Mary icon which she sought in another room, brought the icon for the others to see as she talked about her relationship with it. She shared how the more she gazed at the icon the more she was the child held by Mary—the closer was their bond, which she explained at length. The group applauded Estelle. This was a day for cheering, if only virtually.

Whereupon Francine brought forth something, "I have wanted to share, especially after our trip to Paris, our tour of Chartres cathedral. But now, finally, today is the day. My topic is church architecture and brain hemispheres."

Francine talked about information that had long been with her, from the 1984 book *The Human Mind and the Mind of God: Theological Promise in Brain Research* by James B. Ashbrook (1926-1999), in which Ashbrook, a Methodist theologian, saturated himself with split-brain research available at the time, and combined that information with his background in historical theology to compare the architecture of two famous Christian churches to help understand the East-West thousand-year split in Christianity that happened in 1054; a long-ago fragmentation in Christianity.

Francine explained, "Ashbrook applied brain-hemisphere information to the churches St. Sophia and Chartres. St. Sophia church with its massive dome, (now known as *Hagia Sophia*—Holy Wisdom) in Istanbul (formerly Constantinople) built by Greek Orthodox Christianity in the 6th century. Eventually, it became a mosque and then a museum. In July, 2020, after 86 years as a museum, Hagia Sophia again became a functioning mosque. The second church Ashbrook looked at is Western Christianity's Roman Catholic Chartres cathedral outside Paris with two spires of unequal heights poking dramatically into the sky.

"Ashbrook speculated that the drastic dissimilarity between the churches' architecture reflected differences between Christianity's Eastern Mediterranean and Western Roman approaches to religion/spirituality. He conjectured the architectural differences reflected the East-West sides of Christianity's relationship with brain hemisphere differences. Ashbrook found the God of Eastern Greek Christianity right-minded as revealed in its dome; the Western Latin God left-minded as shown in its spires. The authority of the Greeks derived from mysticism. For the Latins, authority derived from rationalism.

"Ashbrook said Eastern Christianity had too much vision and not enough sight, while Western Christianity had too much inquiry and not enough context. He concluded that neither the dome-like mind or the spire-like mind was adequate by itself."

CHAPTER TWENTY-ONE

Christian Fragmentation, 1054

Francine gave a brief history lesson, reading from her notes, "By 1054 relations between West and East were so contentious that the Roman Pope excommunicated the Greek Patriarch in Constantinople, who in turn anathematized (condemned) the Pope. This angry time came to be called The Great Schism, but is now often referred to as the East-West Schism.

"The estrangement didn't happen overnight. It was a long time in the making. Religious politics and power plays, geographic distances with difficult and lengthy travel were part of the split, so were cultural and language differences. When reading the early history of Christianity, one cannot avoid reading about "Greek and Latin fathers" of the church, which does not necessarily indicate an antagonistic division but rather a language/cultural difference which existed from the very early days of Christianity.

"Perhaps the Christian East-West rupture became inevitable in 395 A.D. when Emperor Theodosius (the Great) divided the Roman Empire between his two sons. What followed was that the Latin Roman Catholic Church of the West and the Greek Orthodox Church of the East went down different paths politically and theologically and for the next centuries the crack between them continued to widen until there was an abyss, and the official break came.

"What were their different paths? According to historical theologian Ashbrook, the Greek-speaking Church of the East tended more toward right-hemisphere, mystical/experiential Christianity, whereas the Latin-speaking Roman Catholic Church of the West cultivated more left-hemisphere, analytical/belief-based Christianity.

"Today, Western Christianity is made up of Catholic and Protestant denominations. Eastern Christianity is in the Balkans, Eastern Europe, Asia Minor, the Middle East, Northeastern Africa and southern India. Each and all originate in Christ.

"What is the status between East-West Christianity today? Over the centuries there have been and continue to be ongoing gestures of reconciliation. A statement from the Second Vatican Council (1962-1965) expresses words of understanding, appreciation and reconciliation with Eastern Christianity:

> In the investigation of revealed truth, East and West have used different methods and approaches in understanding and proclaiming divine things. It is hardly surprising, then, if sometimes one tradition has come nearer than the other to an apt appreciation of certain aspects of a revealed mystery, or has expressed them in a clearer manner. As a result, these various theological formulations are often to be considered as complementary rather than conflicting.[11]

"Complementary rather than conflicting is how the two sides of the brain optimally work together. Understanding complementary characteristics may have prevented Christianity's split in the first place between Greek and Latin cultural differences. But this was not the case at the time. Perhaps today, with increasing appreciation for cultural diversity and complementarity, reunion is possible.

"Reconciliation between Christian East and West continued in 1965, when Pope Paul VI in Rome, and Patriarch Athenagoras in

---

[11] Second Vatican Council documents, *Decree on Ecumenism*, III, 17.

Constantinople, each, in separate ceremonies, withdrew the excommunications and anathemas of many centuries. More healing was sought when Pope John Paul II in May 1999 visited Romania; in 2001 he became the first Pope to visit Greece in 1291 years; then went to Ukraine and Serbia. He wanted also to visit Belarus, and Russia, but unresolved difficulties made this impossible.

"Pope Benedict XVI in November 2006, signed the Common Declaration in Turkey with Patriarch Bartholomew I, which reads in part "We give thanks to the Author of all that is good, who allows us once again, in prayer and in dialogue, to express the joy we feel as brothers and to renew our commitment to move towards full communion."

"On June 29, 2008, Pope Benedict XVI and Patriarch Bartholomew I, together celebrated Mass, the liturgy of the solemnity of Saints Peter and Paul in St. Peter's Basilica. In June, 2010, Pope Benedict traveled to Cyprus to promote interfaith dialogue and closer ties between the Catholic and Orthodox churches. In September 2010 the international Roman Catholic-Orthodox theological dialogue commission met in Vienna.

"Pope Francis, in his earliest days of being Pontiff in March of 2013, spoke of wanting to make efforts to further reconcile the nearly 1,000-year estrangement between Eastern and Western Christianity. At the inaugural Mass of Francis, Orthodox Ecumenical Patriarch Bartholomew I, was in attendance."

Francine concluded, "It makes sense to me that Christianity today will not be completely renewed until the East and West are in full communion. I only know that all religions and branches of religion must deal with left and right brain hemisphere elements, for this is human biology. Christianity is no exception. East and West branches of Christianity are not outside this reality."

And then, as though Francine had a resurgence of energy, she wanted to continue her monologue, "East and West share an absolute bond in Christ, but there are different interpretations and understandings about what Christ brought to humanity. I see this in the area of salvation theology.

"Surely, I am boring you and need not continue, except that I truly want to share this with you." The zoom friends applauded, encouraging

Francine to begin her next topic. Social distancing from Covid made them hungry for "meaty" talk.

CHAPTER TWENTY-TWO

Salvations

Francine, with notes, began, "A principal salvation explanation in Western Christianity is the idea that Jesus "saved" us by dying on the Cross. This salvation theology has a juridical base; it is based on law; the administration of justice. I see it as a rational left-hemisphere explanation that uses analogy, which is a right-hemisphere association, to make its case.

"Jesus paid a price for our salvation, is based on the premise that human beings owe God a great debt, which we can't repay because we are sinners, prone to "miss the target" of being close to God with our limited, flawed, incomplete personalities. Jesus, a fully divinized sinless human, freely sacrificed his life to pay the debt we all owe God. This is the idea in a nutshell.

"This idea of redemption/salvation is largely tied to Anselm of Canterbury (1033-1109), born in Aosta, an Alpine town. He became a Benedictine monk, abbot, ecclesiastical statesman, pastor, champion of the church, philosopher, brilliant theologian, father of scholastic theology, and doctor of the church. He also had some education in law.

"Anselm's title "father of scholastic theology" means he is regarded as the first Catholic theologian to rigorously use a rational approach to understand what Christ brought to humanity. Though he was not as systematic in his writing as Thomas Aquinas would later be, he set the stage for the arduous, meticulous, rational approach of Thomas and later theologians.

"Anselm was trying to make clear why or what was accomplished in the death of Jesus. He attempts to answer these questions by using "proofs" (logical explanations) because Christians had asked him to do so; also to make rational statements about Christianity for non-Christians; and to undo an old idea that Jesus paid a ransom to the devil to buy back humanity for God. I suggest the old idea that humanity enslaved itself by selling itself into the possession of the devil, and that Jesus paid the price to the devil to set humanity free, may originally have been an analogy, a figurative idea which devolved into a literal interpretation.

"I find it plausible that in attempting to undo this old idea about Satan, Anselm uses another analogy based on feudal laws which existed at the time. One such German feudal law worked like this: instead of being punished by incarceration, someone who had dishonored a member of the nobility could pay a fine (*Wergeld*). I suggest Anselm's theological use of the feudal idea was to illustrate that the perfection and supremacy of God ought to be acknowledged by all His creatures, and that a creature who sins refuses that submission and thus violates God's "honor." Quite simply, Jesus paid a "fine" to keep humanity from being imprisoned by our wrongheadedness which dishonors God.

"This salvation theology that Jesus paid a fine is still a dominant Western Christian explanation of what Jesus did for humanity. However, there can be a snag in this understanding if one does not appreciate that an analogy may have been used to make a point. Using a single-minded, literal approach to the analogy makes this argument problematic. A literalist approach makes God seem petty; having the need to be "honored."

"Viewed in this way, the "payment" view of Jesus' sacrifice can be a burden to anyone who already feels wearied by life's complexities and difficulties. Then, this view of a needy, demanding God is not helpful. However, if this salvation theory is speaking figuratively, not literally, God is not a petty tyrant, and the primary relationship we have with Jesus is not one of guilty horror that we made him die. Eastern Christianity offers another version of salvation.

Salvation in the Eastern Christian view concentrates less upon the offense against God of human sin and more upon the bad effects of sin upon us. It sees Gods as not so much offended as concerned to raise human beings to the highest possible level, when they have fallen to a low level, which is a kind of sickness.[12]

"We've only to pay attention to daily news reports to realize humanity is sick in ways and needs healing. We've only to pay attention to our own personal limitations and shortcomings to know we need psychological healing.

"The Eastern Christian notion is that each of us has the potential to be deified, to become participants in divine nature, *theosis*, to become Christlike, Godlike, to develop our God-given potential, the contribution we can uniquely make to life. The idea is that Jesus paved the Way; as fully-evolved cosmic consciousness; universal path to psychological healing and all kinds of fulfillment.

"And yes, it is healthy to remember the price human Jesus paid, which opens this door of healing hope for us, which the Western Christian salvation analogy upholds.

"The Eastern idea of *theosis,* and the Western explanation that "Jesus died for our sins," are two sides of the same coin—complementary theologies. The Western approach is based on justice. The Eastern, on psychology (psyche, soul-healing). The two together explain and expand more fully what each alone has to offer."

The Brunch Bunch tossed Francine's ideas around. Francine apologized for her lengthy explanation, assured by her friends that what she'd given them was most welcome—exactly the kind of stimulating talk they missed because of social isolation during this Covid time. Thanking Francine for giving them something to chew on, to bite into, speaking metaphorically, figuratively.

The Zoom session was fine, yet the friends regretted not eating together, whereupon Estelle suggested their next gathering be lunch in a park, bring your own lunch, eating together while social-distancing in a

---

[12] Stephen Thomas, *Deification in the Eastern Orthodox Tradition: A Biblical Perspective* (Piscataway NJ: Gorgias Press, 2007), p. 7.

park pavilion as the Lunch Bunch instead of the Brunch Bunch. The others applauded approval.

CHAPTER TWENTY-THREE

Pettiness-Anger-Blame

Meanwhile, Sherry hadn't recently seen Justin. She knew a plump commercial real estate deal was underway, most unusual in the pandemic, which was time-intensive for Justin, but she also wondered whether their intense evening with split-brain information was a turn-off for him.

She wished she was back on a university campus where rich, complex conversations were commonplace. Francine and Dee were available for intense conversation, but she wanted people more her age who may not have the depth of knowledge of Dee and Francine, but were satisfying in other ways.

Sherry lived daily with anxiety that Francine would not live much longer. Recently, Francine gave up driving, as glaucoma was slowly stealing her peripheral vision. On occasion, Francine expressed gratitude for having read extensively when younger, as her eyes and stamina could no longer do that. Sherry could tell there was an urgency in Francine to share with others what she'd put together over her lifetime.

So much about Sandshell was right for Sherry, yet she wondered if a more metropolitan area wouldn't be more appealing; yet, those in large cities had to stay at home because of Covid—and she knew her good fortune of being in a home at the beach. Strangely, very strangely, Cynthia and Quinn, their relationship, their dogs and The Merriweather School in common, seemed more satisfactory than Sherry's life at the moment; she didn't want a pet.

Sherry was shocked to realize she felt sinister pleasure when Cynthia told her of Charles's worries about his job, Patrick coming to work at the furniture store in Clarksdale, for she knew Charles and Kendal moved from St. Louis to a much smaller town and life wasn't ideal there either; just as she was now living a somewhat unsatisfactory life.

Sherry felt unsavory pleasure when learning about Dee losing a chunk of her work on Jesus' parables in a computer glitch. Sherry knew enough about depth psychology to recognize her *shadow* in these sinister reactions to others' difficulties.

Could she help others accept their shadow issues when her own were roaring around in her just now? She prayed in earnest about this streak of petty meanness she saw in herself, of which she was ashamed. She could not inwardly empathize with Dee's stress over her computer loss, though she outwardly said the right words. Sherry was trapped in her own displeasures at the moment. Dee had been unbelievably forthright when she told of what seemed a catastrophe when a large part of Jesus' parables vanished from her computer.

Dee explained her computer distress, "I had not thought to save this work on an external drive. How could I have been so careless, thick-headed, mindless. And where was God in this—omniscient, omnipresent, omnipotent God who couldn't intervene in so small a matter, or didn't do so because the problem was so unimportant?"

Dee's body was in turmoil, her mind overwhelmed, pages and pages gone, not retrievable despite help from an expert. Perhaps they needed to find someone with more expertise. Dee was angry, blaming. She knew it was total absurdity to react as she did, which was that when somebody is in utter distress, as with Jesus at his crucifixion, "the Father" was not available. She agreed it was insanity to be thinking such. However, her insane idea went like this: Jesus was left to suffer by himself, "forsaken."

Dee wrestled with the possibility that chance and good-luck bad-luck rule daily existence—not deity. Or deity is merely chance and luck. Dee's temporary bitterness, Dee could scarcely believe herself, extended even to Mary, mother of Jesus, who from Dee's childhood seemed ever tender, loving, caring. Couldn't Mary have reminded Dee to save her computer work more securely? It is said, 'All things work to the good for those who are called by God.' (Rm 8:28) *Really?* Dee thought angrily.

Maybe no one was to blame, not even Dee, which goes back to chance and luck. Gradually, Dee came to entertain the possibility that something positive could come from losing many pages of text, though she could not yet imagine what that might be. Much like the possibility that eventual good would come from Covid-19, despite the suffering and deaths, economic distress and overall inconveniences. And what might that good be?

Dee well understood Simon Peter answering Jesus, "To whom shall we go?" after Jesus asked the twelve apostles if they were going to leave him as others had. Dee had no other place to go with her concerns, the fears and anxieties of everyday living, her need for something Ultimate with or without this computer calamity.

She had an automatic reaction to pray when situations went wrong, as well as when all was fine. Where would she go psychologically, in her thoughts, in her feelings, without this lifetime habit of connection with something Ultimate? She needed to fuss, complain, argue, blame, disagree, for even then she was relating, she was in relationship.

The word Israel means "to wrestle or contend with God." Dee had often done that in her gender confusion, but with that no longer distressing her, she hadn't the need to regularly have it out with the Ultimate in the universe.

In the midst of her computer anger, Dee had a one-scene sleeptime dream of a bundle of six or so peeled eggs, hard-boiled, ready for her. Eggs symbolize potential for new life. Perhaps the aftermath of her computer disaster was bringing new potential. For that, she could only be grateful. Awake, she interacted with the dream and found she wanted to embrace the eggs, hugging them close to her—close in her awareness.

Dee shared all of this with Zach who sympathized greatly with her plight, knew a computer retrieval person who was able to recover some of what she'd lost, and suggest she purchase a new computer, which she did. A computer is a machine that wears out, becomes obsolete, malfunctions, needs to be backed-up. Dee was back on track with The Ultimate, a new computer, her project of the parables. She forgave herself, and Ultimate Itself.

What good came of this? She would likely never again forget to back-up her work, which was coming together in a smoother, better way now than before. Foremost, she experienced a stronger relationship with God, who as "Father," had long been problematic for her.

She now felt she could be thoroughly candid, hold nothing back, express anger and doubt, while steadfast presence remained. God could not be insulted out of existence. God knew her anger and doubt anyway, which was best not hidden from her own awareness. Even in her angry grief she had been in relationship with the whole god-thing, which is about relationship she now knew, stronger than before.

Estelle recently mentioned grandson Dexter's observation that he and his friends feel "empty." Estelle commented, "Sometimes forlorn emptiness or depletion can be a prelude to being filled by the presence of God, or it can also become chronic depression. She remembered in *Mere Christianity*, C.S. Lewis connected *kenosis* and *theosis*, 'The Son of Man became a man to enable men to become sons of God.' Emptiness can become Fullness.

Estelle reflected on the aphorism "Let go and let God" in AA. She knew she had to let-go of her egoistic trying to get Dexter past using psychedelics and marijuana. She had to let go of Dexter, and put him in God's hands so as to be filled with God's presence instead of chemically manipulating himself into different states of relaxation, awareness, consciousness.

Estelle puzzled over something Reggie occasionally said, beginning when he was much younger, "We all *get* to die." Was he being sarcastic? Was death a relief from underlying depression? A privilege? A necessary evil? Estelle never understood this utterance of Reggie. She had the feeling he was a deeper person than she ever appreciated.

Sherry never forgot her teenage psychedelic experience. She was not tempted to repeat that now when going through a down-time. What she was presently learning is that there are pockets of adolescent arrogance still alive in her; the feeling that she has the answers to life's questions. However, she now sees ever more clearly that the need for adult humility never ends. It's easy to assume we know more than we do, at any age.

CHAPTER TWENTY-FOUR

Brother Lawrence

Quinn stopped being concerned that Vatican II documents have only one mention of the contemplative life in the index, but he couldn't stop wondering whether church hierarchy seriously pondered why the young seekers of the '60s sought gurus and Asian religion rather than Christianity. Their seeking was going on at the same time Vatican II was taking place.

He knew Jesuit, Karl Rahner, the German theologian who died in 1984, had been hugely influential preparing for Vatican II as well as during the proceedings. Knowing this about Rahner, Quinn felt certain Rahner's comment that the Christian of the future will be a mystic or not be Christian at all must have been present to some degree during the Vatican sessions because of Rahner's high profile presence.

Or, did Rahner's comment about future Christians being mystics, made years after Vatican II, come from his later reflections on what Vatican II produced alongside headline news that told of the search of the young for Asian spirituality, not Christianity. Was Rahner a prophet who saw incongruence between the track the Vatican was on and what the adults of tomorrow were searching for spiritually.

Quinn knew enough about Rahner the theologian to know he felt to be human is to be in relationship with God; to be inseparable from God; to have genuine experiences of God ultimately rooted in spiritual existence, even in everyday activities to dwell in encounters with the mystery of God; that modern men and women were interested in their interior life; that being human was about being in companionship with God.

Quinn had read about Christian mysticism in some of the extensive writings of Bernard McGinn, theologian and scholar, but was particularly drawn to the very thin, homespun book, *The Practice of the Presence of God*, which contains conversations and letters of Brother Lawrence (born Nicholas Herman in French Lorraine) who became a monk in 1666 in Paris at the age of 18, and died at 80. Brother Lawrence worked in a clanging, banging monastery kitchen, where he said, he ever and always felt the presence of God. Brother Lawrence does not tell of experiencing exalted states of awareness or unusual happenings. His mysticism was simple everyday tranquility, inner peace.

Those who knew the monk observed that in the greatest hurry of business in the kitchen Brother Lawrence still preserved his recollection and heavenly-mindedness. He was never hasty nor loitering, but did each thing in its season, with an even, uninterrupted composure and tranquility of spirit. Brother Lawrence wrote that he had no will but that of God, which he endeavored to accomplish in all things, and noted there is not in the world a life more sweet and delightful than that of continual conversation with God, claiming that work time is not different from prayer time. That in the noise and clatter of the kitchen, while several persons are at the same time calling for different things, he possessed God in as great tranquility as if he was upon his knees at the blessed sacrament.

Quinn desired everyday tranquility, not stigmata, or levitations, trances, apparitions, visions, non-ordinary mind states, speaking in tongues, or seeing purple as Cynthia told him Dee does. Quinn wanted a caring cosmic companion, which he found when he was young, in Christ.

Now, working with nontraditional students, Quinn preferred serenity to offset the anxieties and tsunami emotions in students. He knew about, but had not read the book, *Abandonment to Divine Providence,* whose title tells the content of this 18th century book written by French Jesuit Jean-Pierre de Caussade. Quinn had a formula: release concerns, priorities and plans to Creation Itself, and contentment will be yours whilst you do your part to take care of everyday matters and make the world better, cooperating with grace.

Leafing through the tiny book of Brother Lawrence, Quinn found he'd underlined:

"I say again, let us enter unto ourselves . . . Those who have the gale of the Holy Spirit go forward even in sleep. If the vessel of our soul is still tossed with winds and storms, let us awake the Lord, who reposes in it, and He will quickly calm the sea."

Quinn had found he wasn't meant to be a priest but knew he had the desire for, and the capacity to live in the moment in constant contact, conversation and companionship with Divine Presence because he did truly align his existence with such the best he knew how. He had never found anything or anyone else with which to align his existence. He knew he'd want anyone he might marry to understand this about him. But then, re-considered this conviction. No one but he himself need know about his deep longing for what is intimately Incomprehensible.

CHAPTER TWENTY-FIVE

Baby Matti—Abortion

Meanwhile, at Montel Furniture store in Clarksdale KS, all was going well with Patrick Montel now part of the work force. Indeed, Marc Montel was, of course, owner and boss, but Patrick's employment greatly improved Marc's life leaving him less time-pressured, and relieved wife Julia of guilt about having never worked alongside Marc at the store, but chose instead to be busy with activities in the community, most especially therapeutic "Tiny Things" at Golden Acres convalescent home.

"Tiny Things" was thriving as a town treasure with several hundred miniature figurines donated by locals who made purchases when travelling and donated them to the ever-growing collection. Few knew that "Tiny Things" came to life in her children's sand pile in the family backyard when Julia, in desperation, engaged in physically creating scenes in the sand that helped alleviate her anger toward birth mother, Matti.

Julia had learned about the field of sandplay therapy in her psychiatric training as a nurse, implemented it in her own way in the backyard sandpile, and then adapted it to non-sand conditions for the residents in Golden Acres who were fascinated by the tiny figurines. Whether suffering with dementia, loss from strokes, depression or other impairments, the objects attracted participants.

As Julia learned more about brain-hemisphere differences, she felt the tiny figures tapped *into* right-hemisphere operations. She was now gathering data with medical residents at the regional behavioral center outside of town, to see if her hunch might be so. Seniors in high school continued to help those who needed assistance with the tiny things. Each session began with thorough handwashing of each participant so that figurines, hands and environment, were kept clean. This practice began long before the Covid-19 pandemic. Now, wearing face masks and fewer residents per session to allow for social-distancing, became the norm. Overall, Golden Acre residents and students both benefit from the interaction between them.

With the return of Patrick and Brooke, two of the three Montel children had returned to Clarksdale. Julia could scarcely grasp this good turn of events. Perhaps eldest Benjamin might one day return as a psychiatrist in the regional behavioral center.

Most recently, Patrick and wife Brooke became parents of baby girl Matti. Matti Montel. They liked the resonance of the name, knowing the name Matti was that of Julia's birth mother.

When younger, Julia would have been irritated by the name, however, at this time in her life Julia was actually pleased. It had taken years for Julia to have a positive attitude toward the reality of her biological mother. Sandplay in Julia's own backyard had helped heal her, and then, tiny things with the elderly and infirm had become her lifelong passion. All things can work for good.

Meanwhile, in Sandshell the pandemic Lunch Bunch enjoyed being together, eating together under a pavilion in a park. Why hadn't they thought of gathering like this sooner. Dee shared news of baby girl Matti in Clarksdale, which triggered the topic of abortion when the significance of the name Matti was explained to the group by Dee, as the name of Julia's birth mother. Everyone had met Julia at the wedding of Charles and Kendal in Clarksdale.

It wasn't a contentious abortion discussion in the park, but a look at the volatile issue of abortion by four Catholic women, Dee, Estelle, Monique and Francine who concluded that making a personal individual decision compared to legislating a decision for a group, a community, a state, or the nation, are far different matters.

Though one might personally never darken the door of an abortion clinic, or take a pill to terminate a pregnancy, does an individual have the right or the obligation to forbid others from having a regulated medically safe abortion rather than trying to terminate a pregnancy oneself with sometimes unintended lethal consequences, or pay an unregulated somebody who will do this.

Outlawing abortions will not create a perfect world, just like outlawing liquor during days of Prohibition did not create a perfect world, but fostered other unseemly situations. The conversation looked at abortions from various angles. There are now various effective means of birth control, which is one way of lessening the need for abortion. Being smarter about the difference between committed love and the sex drive is important even at an early age. In general, the human condition is too varied for a one-size-fits-all-solution to arguments about abortion.

However, and above all, legislating a problem out of existence isn't possible, and only creates more problems. Giving simple answers to complex questions is not helpful, just as giving complex answers to simple questions is not of benefit. As a nation we need to grow into subtle, nuanced understanding, otherwise we can be prone to short-sighted remedies, not real solutions.

The women knew the knotty issue of abortion was, of course, a matter of conscience, desperation, and countless other components, with well-intentioned opinions on each side. Yet, in the end, decisions whether to keep legal abortion or abolish legalization on local, state or federal levels would be made. And this is not easy. Morality and legality are not always the same.

That morning, it was again obvious to everyone in the group, including Francine, that she was increasingly eager to share information with the others because of problems with her eyes. She felt the day would come when activities for her would be seriously compromised because of diminished vision.

She had a copy for each of what she wanted to talk about which she didn't believe she'd ever shared with any of them. It was once again about the divided brain, which she found a powerful part of psychotherapy.

Yes, including married couple clients (such as Kelly and Paul) who increasingly realize they are opposites in the way they interpret situations, approach life and each other. Francine explained, "A married couple I'm working with is beginning to look at themselves and each other through the lens of brain-hemispheres. On this sheet is a list tied to the work of experts, authorities, scholars, compiled early in the days of split-brain research. This list has appeared in various books, including a book on androgyny. Why would an author put this list in her book on androgyny?"

Dee was struck deep in her being by this question! She was momentarily (but not visibly, she hoped) overcome by a physical hot-flash; the memory of her own gender struggles still burned inside. But why would an author on androgyny put a list about split-brain in her book? Francine had written her own comments on the sheet she gave her friends.

CHAPTER TWENTY-SIX

Split Brain and Androgyny

Below, is a list dealing with brain-hemispheres, which is included in a book on gender, *Androgyny: the opposites within*, published and republished in 1976, 1989, 2000, written by June Singer (1920-2004), an analyst trained in the psychology of C.G. Jung. It may be strange this information on brain-hemisphere differences is in a book on gender, but then, Jung himself spoke often of psychological feminine elements in a male (anima) and psychological masculine elements in a female (animus). It is known that the male body has some female hormones and the female body has some male hormones.

This list of the characteristics of two modes of knowing was assembled by Robert E. Ornstein in his book, *The Psychology of Consciousness* (New York NY: Harcourt Brace Jovanovich, Inc. 1977, p. 37). Ornstein's work was a spinoff from the split-brain research begun by Roger Sperry and further explored by others. It is in the 2000 edition of Singer's book on androgyny, page 158.

Who Proposed It?

Many sources	Day	Night
Blackburn	Intellectual	Sensuous
Oppenheimer	Time, History	Eternity, Time-lessness
Deikman	Active	Receptive
Polyani	Explicit	Tacit
Levy, Sperry	Analytic	Gestalt
Domhoff	Right side of body	Left side of body
Many sources	Left hemisphere	Right hemisphere
Bogen	Propositional	Appositional
Lee	Lineal	Nonlineal
Luria	Sequential	Simultaneous
Semmes	Focal	Diffuse
I Ching	The Creative: heaven	The Receptive: earth
I Ching	masculine, Yang	feminine, Yin
I Ching	Light	Dark
I Ching	Time	Space
Many sources	Verbal	Spatial
Many sources	Intellectual	Intuitive
Vedanta	Buddhi	Manas
Jung	Causal	Synchronicity
Bacon	Argument	Experience

Francine explained, "This list, assembled in the early days of studying brain-hemisphere differences, reflects various labels used to designate the brain hemispheres, which you know I describe as dancing partners working in-synch back and forth across the corpus callosum. Our task, it seems to me is to recognize and appreciate the unique characteristics of each hemisphere and at this time in history to re-cognize the valuable contributions of the right-hemisphere which has been devalued for far too long."

Estelle inserted, "Brain hemispheres remind me of the question whether life is a problem to be solved or a mystery to be lived. Seems to me the answer is that life is full of problems to be solved as well as living out grand mystery. This is the crux of being alive and always will be. To me, this old philosophical question can be tied to what is now known about brain-hemispheres today."

Monique astutely observed that brain-hemispheres politically divide this country today, trapped in flux and upheaval over brain approach and don't know it. "Justin says he and Sherry talk about brain hemisphere difference. I tell myself, 'Brain difference since the 60s is the reason we divide today.'"

Monique had just revealed something about Justin and Sherry the others did not know. Did Monique mean to do this, or did she innocently blunder into telling? But then, Justin knew he was talking with his tell-all mother. So, what was his motive sharing his Sherry conversation about brain hemispheres with his mother? Did Justin feel he was doing therapy with Sherry? Dee wondered whether Cynthia knew about Sherry and Justin.

Dee was absorbing Monique's revelation about Sherry and Justin when Francine shocked her with talk of split-brain information in the book on androgyny, unnerving Dee when Francine asked, 'Why would an author put this list on brain hemisphere labels in her book on androgyny?" In her discomfort, Dee sought to deflect the emotions going on inside her by posing a remark in defense of what the left-hemisphere has brilliantly provided through the centuries, as author McGilchrist points out in the latest edition of his book, *The Master and His Emissary*.

> I do not underestimate the importance of the left hemisphere's contribution to all that humankind has achieved . . . It is a wonderful servant, but a very poor master. . . The right hemisphere, though it is not dependent on the left hemisphere in the same way that the left is on the right, nonetheless *needs* it in order to achieve its full potential.[13]

Dee silently pondered further McGilchrist's ideas that those who believe religion is mistaken or does more harm than good, must recognize religion's many valuable and beautiful contributions. Likewise, the

---

[13] McGilchrist, *The Master and His Emissary,* 2019, p. 437.

Enlightenment in 1700s Europe, though too narrowly focused on reason and science as having all the answers, did on the upside, help moderate superstition.

Dee was pleased to remember invaluable quotes from sidewalk humanities professor Oriana that expressed the value of properly intentioned metaphor which seems to reside in right-hemisphere comprehension. And another quote about science and religion.

> It would be nice if people were to understand that science is a special exercise in perceiving the world without metaphor, and that, powerful though it is, it doesn't function as a guide to those very large aspects of experience that can't be perceived except through metaphor.[14]

> Science and religion do not have to be incompatible: One need not be wrong for the other to be right.[15] All human beings have a brain, and all of these brains work in a very similar fashion. So if we are ever going to get a sense of the universal aspects of religion, then the brain might be the best place to start.[16]

Dee was grateful for Oriana who refers to God as "Grace." Recently on the telephone, Oriana talked about making a decision based on whether it seemed Grace indicated this or that. Dee almost said, "Grace who?" until she remembered Oriana calls God, "Grace."

But now, no longer lost in her own thoughts, Dee realized Francine was passing out another sheet of paper to her friends.

---

[14] Francis Spufford, *Unapologetic: Why, Despite Everything, Christianity Can Still Make Surprising Emotional Sense*, London UK: Faber and Faber Limited, 2012), p. 222.
[15] Newberg, *Why God Won't Go Away*, p. 173.
[16] Newberg, *Why God Won't Go Away*, p. 176.

CHAPTER TWENTY-SEVEN

Two Authors

**Francine comparing two books
one written by a neuroanatomist female recovering from a stroke
and the other by a college professor who is a monk**

Francine explained, "The male, Martin Laird, a member of the religious Order of St. Augustine, associate professor in the department of theology and religious studies at Villanova University, wrote the book, *Into the Silent Land: The Practice of Contemplation* in 2006. Below, I use comments from Laird's book and follow each statement with a parallel remark of neuroanatomist Jill Bolte Taylor's description of her stroke experience in her 2008 book, *My Stroke of Insight*.

"Taylor, in 1996 at the age of 37, suffered a stroke in the left-hemisphere of her brain which left her debilitated. It took her eight years to recover. She poignantly describes the defining features of each brain hemisphere as she experienced her left- hemisphere functions shut down during her stroke and her increasing awareness of right-hemisphere functions. Taylor writes,

Within four brief hours, I watched my mind completely deteriorate in its ability to process all stimulation coming in through my senses. This rare form of hemorrhage rendered me completely disabled whereby I could not walk, talk, read, write, or recall any aspects of my life.[17] . . . The harder I tried to concentrate, the more fleeting my ideas seemed to be. Instead of finding answers and information, I met a growing sense of peace . . . tranquil euphoria . . . an expanding sense of grace . . . "being at one" with the universe.[18]

"I interpret Laird's use of Mt. Zion as the right-brain hemisphere, his use of weather around Mt. Zion as describing left-brain functions. Here then, is my interface between a monk and a neuroscientist. Laird's words are followed by descriptions of Taylor's experience."

Laird: "Union with God is not something that needs to be acquired but realized." (p. 10)

Taylor realized, experienced, right-hemisphere functions as her left-hemisphere functions were increasingly disabled. She was not trying to make this happen.

Laird: "When the mind is held by silence, an open field of awareness emerges as the unifying ground of All." (p. 11)

Taylor became silent inside as left-hemisphere language centers were shutting down. "Those little voices, that brain chatter delightfully silent." (p.42)

Laird: "Our deepest identity is like Mount Zion, unshakeable, unchanging, eternal . . . Our changing thoughts, feelings, moods, impulses, cravings, inklings, are like so much weather on Mount Zion... For a lifetime we have taken this weather—our thoughts and feelings—to be ourselves. The more we realize we are one with God the more we become ourselves, just as we are, just as we were created to be." (pp. 14-17)

Taylor writes: "Without my left brain available . . . my consciousness ventured unfettered into the peaceful bliss of my divine right mind." (p.61) Taylor makes similar comments on the internet TED website.

---

[17] Taylor, *My Stroke of Insight*, p. 11.
[18] Taylor, *My Stroke of Insight*, p. 41.

Laird: "A mountain does not determine what sort of weather is happening but witnesses all the weather that comes and goes. The weather is our thoughts, changing moods, feelings, impressions, reactions, our character." (p. 86)

In the eight years **Taylor** was healing from the stroke, she was aware of the impact of thoughts. "I don't have to think thoughts that bring me pain." (p. 147)

Laird: "There is a deeper core that is utterly free and vast and silent, that no thought or feeling has ever entered." (p. 87)

Taylor writes, "As the language centers in my left hemisphere grew increasingly silent. . . I was comforted by an expanding sense of grace . . . all-knowingness, a "being at one" with the universe." (p. 41)

Laird: "The grace-filled dynamic of silence shows us how uncluttered, spacious, still, and calm our awareness is and has always been, majestic as a mountain." (p. 89)

Taylor writes, "Deep within a sacred cocoon with a silent mind and a tranquil heart, I felt the enormousness of my energy lift." (p. 63)

Laird: "The mind [left-hemisphere] is always doing something, so give it something to do: let it quietly repeat a short phrase, or a prayer word." (pp. 51, 35)

Taylor makes recommendations, including prayer, where we intentionally replace unwanted thought patterns with a mantra or chosen set of thought patterns. (pp. 169-170)

~~~~

Francine concluded: "Laird's figurative use of the weather around Mt. Zion compared to Mt. Zion itself, cleverly, poignantly, alludes to the mental struggle in the human personality. Before neuroscience, spiritual literature sometimes referred to this dilemma as the thinking mind or discursive reason versus the silent vastness of the heart."

Francine using Mt. Zion in this way stoked Dee's ideas of Christianity as myth, as the story of spirit and matter coming together in the incarnation, as the story of resurrection, those times in life when we are crucified

by circumstances, situations, people, even our own personality but survive such crucifixions to become stronger, wiser. The Christian story is
one in which God suffers so that incarnation and resurrection are part of
everyday life. God is in all and all is in God, always and ever. Religion at
its best helps us know God is with us as we struggle.

Hearing words about a God who submits to suffer, Monique cham-
pioned her comments weeks ago about Chagall's art related to Christ's
suffering. Monique herself was a puzzle. Just when it appeared she wasn't
listening, she had been. This was often the case with Monique. As
Monique spoke about Chagall, Estelle was thinking of Mother Mary, as
cosmic feminine energy.

Dee never stopped being impressed with author McGilchrist's ideas,
and why she had to keep re-reading his thick book. She was fascinated
by the story behind the title of his book, *The Master and His Emissary.*

The title of McGilchrist's book comes from a story about a wise self-
less spiritual master who ruled over a small flourishing expanding domain. The ruler carefully trained trusted emissaries to help him with the
most distant areas of the domain. Eventually, his most trusted emissary,
also the cleverest and most ambitious, increased his own wealth and influence, eventually usurping the master, duping the people, and the domain collapsed in tyranny. McGilchrist says this story illustrates what has
been happening in Western culture, with left-hemisphere brain preference for over the last 500 years or so.

Dee increasingly felt McGilchrist's book was one of the most insightful she had ever read. It informed her passion about the brain-hemispheres. Actually, she didn't have that passion, the passion had her. And
while his book impassioned her, so did working on the parables of Jesus,
which she was completing after the computer calamity nearly derailed her
project permanently. Is it a blessing or a curse to have enduring passions—who knows how many passions she has, Dee wondered about
herself amusedly.

CHAPTER TWENTY-EIGHT

Trapped at the Corners

Fall classes with students online began for Cynthia and Quinn, keeping the two teachers unbelievably busy with almost no time for texting, telephoning, or walking together with Bios and Pixie-Pickett in the park. First-time teacher Cynthia was overwhelmed, ever thinking about, planning, organizing material for second-graders online. "You don't know how difficult, how stressful this is," she told Dee and Zach, "I don't sleep well because I can't stop dealing with school, students, lessons."

It was Dee who suggested Quinn be invited for a second evening of dinner on the Kendrick patio, including Bios and Pixie-Pickett, of course. The patio dinner came to be, with no one wanting to talk about classes, students, or Covid. Libations and lovely finger foods started the evening and wiped away these burdensome topics while plunging the four into another snakepit of conversation.

Politics became the focus of interest in the latest Brunch Bunch gathering; why this nation is so distressingly politically divided. Monique's opinion was that brain-hemisphere difference is the root of the national split which ripples across geographic regions, groups of individuals, and Francine had counseled, "We must remember the brain-hemispheres are not either/or possibilities. Rather, they are optimally like dancing partners in rhythm and harmony with each other." Well, it was agreed there was no bipartisan dancing going on these Covid days.

This evening on the Kendrich patio, Zach sent politics an interesting direction drawing on his napkin the human eye 👁 which he illustrated as he spoke, "It seems to me, people with political extremes whether liberal/progressive or conservative, have little wiggle room. Each is able to see only out of a corner of the eye, whereas people in the center can move out from the middle and across the center and have much greater room in which to ruminate and cogitate—a broader perspective to navigate the waters of reflective understanding, discourse, debate, and healthy compromise, able to see other peoples' points of view. I see those stuck in the end-points as trapped, perhaps steeped in fear, anger or grievance. I know about fear. I never forget my panic attack. I know how powerful fear can be."

Dee was surprised Zach mentioned the panic attack. Cynthia seriously wished he hadn't. Zach elaborated, "I had my own philosophy at that time, that I called "collapse into," which basically meant I endeavored to keep up with responsibilities, take care of things as they turned up, did what I could and then turned the rest over to God. So, how did I get trapped in fear?

"I didn't have a broad enough frame of reference. My philosophy was fine so far as it went, but left-out the unpredictable, what is out of one's control, and I should have known better because Roxanne's death was certainly unexpected, so how could I forget the unexpected, such as not getting a job promotion I felt certain would happen, and didn't."

Zach became quiet, as if he was thinking through something for the first time, or he was perhaps processing the situation at a different level. The moment was quiet except for the sound of the fan overhead doing its job, making the somewhat humid air more livable.

Then, Zach picked-up where he'd left-off, "I don't like the idea of 'hope for the best, expect the worst.' Somehow there's too much fear in that saying, too much pessimism. As I was slowly recovering from the panic attack, I remembered the bible verse, 'Seek *first* the Kingdom of God' (Mt 6:30). *First* indicates priorities. In my 'collapse into' philosophy, "I" was still in first-place, the driver of my efforts, yet if someone asked me whether I keep my own heart beating, my lungs working, blood flowing, cells rejuvenating, I would have to say, 'no.' The autonomic system that runs my body is mostly outside my control, correct?" He looked at biology teacher Quinn for confirmation.

Quinn agreed, "Correct." He elaborated, "The two divisions of the autonomic nervous system are the *sympathetic* in fight or flight, and the *parasympathetic* of rest and digest. Homeostasis is the balance between the two."

Dee was astonished Zach was revealing so much of himself, as he told how the panic attack led to Reggie's suggestion that he look into working with affordable housing which became and remains a most satisfying job involving enough interface with city hall to make it most interesting. He's always been fascinated with politics and his interaction with city hall includes an element of politics.

Dee revealed herself, responding to Zach's revelation about a *first* priority, she said, "I like the hymn words, 'I go before you always, come follow me, and I will give you rest.' I find it reassuring that Divinity leads, paves the way, guides, always—if we can only learn to depend on this."

Zach elaborated more than Dee expected, when he said, "It's about be-coming by following Being. There is no such word as 'do-coming,' but there is be-coming. I tend to be a person driven to *doing* rather than *being*, which can be like having the cart before the horse, though I find life far less stressful when I depend on the lead of Divinity.

"Dee has helped me see we need to *be-come* aware of being lead, develop a sense of *be-longing* to something greater than ourself."

Cynthia was glad for this conversation and wished she could do what they were talking about with her stress over second-graders connected by the internet. She was suffering, really suffering with her job; felt frantic most of the time. She did feel safe and secure with Dee and Zach; living at home; which she wouldn't admit to anyone. She knew she would persevere and endure as a 2nd grade teacher during the pandemic, but wished she could be-come aware of and be-long to what her dad and Dee already seemed to know.

Zach was saying, "It's about Presence from Latin *praesentia*, the fact or condition of being present. Dee has taught me to look at the roots of words. She is often my teacher and I am her cheerleader. Somehow one can come to know, to feel, to experience Presence in all situations, which makes all the difference. The trick is to discern and cooperate with Presence."

Quinn knew that's what Brother Lawrence did many years ago in his clanging, banging monastery kitchen, and thus shared that the monk at the age of eighteen had an extraordinary experience which impacted the rest of his life.

Quinn shared, "One day in the middle of the winter the eighteen-year-old who would become Brother Lawrence saw a dry and leafless tree standing gaunt against the snow, which stirred deep thoughts within him of the change the coming spring would bring when leaves, flowers and fruit would appear, and he received an exalted understanding of the providence and power of God which never left him, and from then on he tried constantly to walk in God's presence."

Quinn looked at Cynthia, stretched his hand on the table towards her seated indirectly across the table from him for social distancing, and said, "This shows the power of nature, and now especially with the virus making nature seem cruel, I think you, me and our dogs need to daily walk in nature and be renewed. Nature can alleviate stress like nothing else; it puts everything into perspective. We should make it a top priority."

CHAPTER TWENTY-NINE

St. John Henry Newman

Cynthia's silence that evening made Quinn acutely aware of Cynthia's upset; she nodded in agreement with his suggestion about a daily walk. He further suggested Cynthia and Pixie-Pickett not meet him and Bios at their usual park, but rather, he and his dog would meet her and her dog here at the Kendrick house and the four would go to a park nearby.

This was Quinn's fourth year to teach. It was Cynthia's first year, complicated by Covid, and Quinn had empathy for Cynthia. His gesture towards Cynthia spoke to Dee, who decided to give him a copy of her now completed commentary on Jesus' parables. She'd given copies to the Brunch Brunch in the park last time they met, but no one had yet given her feedback. She would value comments from Quinn someday. She wanted someone to tell her their reaction to what she'd done with the parables.

Meanwhile, Dee had begun researching St. John Henry Newman (1801-1890), a new saint, canonized October 13, 2019. She found his outer life interesting, converting from an Anglican clergyman to becoming a Roman Catholic, a Roman Catholic priest, eventually named a Cardinal of the church.

Dr. Newman was a scholar-theologian who had taught at Oxford. He was a major part of the spiritual Oxford Movement prior to joining the Roman Catholic church. After his conversion to Roman Catholicism, he wrote about student centers on secular college campuses where Catholic students could gather to know each other, worship together, and enjoy socializing, which are today's Newman Centers at colleges and universities.

Overall, Newman was a person with wide ranging concerns for others, greatly valuing friendships, while knowing isolation and controversy in his decision to become Roman Catholic, as well as on other topics.

Dee's main fascination with Newman was his use of the *illative* sense, which comes from grammar and has to do with introducing or expressing an inference. *Thus* and *therefore* are illative conjunctions. The word illative is from Latin *inferre,* bring in, infer. Newman was interested in the state of mind of *certainty.* For instance, being certain there is a God, what has the individual included leading to such a judgment?

Newman was well acquainted with Formal Logic, and realized logical reasoning with its syllogisms does not answer life's most practical and personal questions. This is where the *illative* sense comes in. He did not have at his fingertips all of the psychological terms and concepts available to us, yet he was tackling the question of how one becomes *certain;* makes up one's mind. Again, how does an individual conclude God exists.

The illative sense suggests *common-sense,* Aristotle's *phronesis,* when what comes into play are converging probabilities, inferences, intuition, hunches, impressions, past experience, innate, instinctual, interior stirrings, the implicit, 'psychological facts,' in his quote below, written in 1870:

> In religious inquiry each of us can speak only for himself, and for himself he has a right to speak. His own experiences are enough for himself, but he cannot speak for others; he cannot lay down the law; he can only bring his own experiences to the common stock of psychological facts . . . he brings together his

reasons, and relies on them, because they are his own, and this is his primary evidence.[19]

It seems, at times Newman promotes individualism, yet this was not at all the case. On one hand, he felt the evolving collective wisdom of the Roman Catholic church was necessary to fully express what Christ brought to humanity. On the other hand, he'd made his own individual decision to become Roman Catholic. In the paragraph above he writes of one's own experiences, reasons, as primary evidence.

Dee felt 'certain' if we could talk with Newman today, he would agree that logic can become rationalism just as science can become scientism, or subjective experience can become individualism. This happens when *a way* of knowing becomes *the way* of knowing, resulting in lopsided understanding, with other ways of knowing undervalued, while the privileged 'way' is overvalued, overused, claims too much.

It seemed to Dee she was back on the topic of practical hermeneutics, how we interpret our experiences, and felt she'd worn the topic out, or it had worn her out. Yet, here she was, having stumbled onto it again, and memories flooded back.

Dee recognized that John Henry Newman valued left-brain Aristotelian logic but he knew it was not the whole story when it comes to human knowing. Dee herself had tried to be rational about her gender confusion which took her nowhere. She also knew Aristotle said there was genius in metaphor, which is more right-brain. It was metaphor that took Dee to herself and began to greatly relieve her gender struggle.

In the same way, Alcoholics Anonymous goes beyond rational argument or scientific findings to help against cravings for alcohol. AA's format helps one experience profound shifts in perspective; perhaps many all-at-once changes, which seems like Newman's illative sense.

Newman concluded one's *conscience* is an important player when converging probabilities come together in the illative sense. In AA, morality is the concern in four of the Twelve Steps. Dee saw wisdom in the old fourfold format she had used with Jesus' parables which includes the moral exponent. Dee reflected on the fact that both reason and science

---

[19] John Henry Newman, *An Essay in Aid of a Grammar of Assent*, (New edition, London, 1892), Chapter 10, p. 385.

need conscience (ethics, morality) to keep them from becoming monstrous.

In Nazi Germany, it may have seemed rational (though atrociously, reprehensibly immoral, evil) to perform scientific experiments on, and exterminate with technological efficiency those persons declared unfit or not valued for one reason or another. Newman included conscience as part of the judgments we make, the conclusions we come to, the certainties we assume.

Dee wanted to stop caring about two-sides of the brain which now felt like old information to her. John Henry Newman's grasp of the illative sense was another piece of affirming information beyond science and rationality. Dee had often wished for a specific term rather than non-science, non-rationality, irrationality, to talk about all-at-once intuitive knowing. She found Newman's 'illative sense' of converging probabilities useful to allude to non-rational, non-scientific processing that goes on in the personality. What might Newman have said if he'd known about the differences between brain-hemispheres?

Dee concluded to herself, *We should not aim too low with our prayer life and miss the target of our entire life, which is centered intimacy, relationship, aligning our life with Spirit's intention for who we can become.*

CHAPTER THIRTY

Transubstantiation

Justin telephoned Sherry after a stretch of weeks of merely perfunctory texts between them. And finally, this evening the two were together on Sherry's tiny balcony, enjoying pre-sunset splendor along with wine, and gourmet food Justin special-ordered and brought. His large-scale commercial real estate deal was now completed. And his birthday had passed. He said he needed to get both of those events out of the way.

Sherry commented, "I understand about the real estate deal, but why your birthday? Why did you need it to pass?"

"I have conflicted feelings about my birthday. My earliest birthday memories are that my mother was more frazzled than usual celebrating the birthdays of Christiane and me. She did it alright, but it was almost as if the family had to pay the price, for she had one more thing she had to do. Christmas wasn't so bad because the real estate market was usually slow before Christmas, but our birthdays were random, unrelated to the market season, and she therefore had to squeeze celebration into everyday complications; just more she had to do.

"However, convoluted-Monique considered my birthday special, which made me wonder how Christiane must have felt. The specialness of my birthday is that it is October 2, the Feast of Guardian Angels. Monique religiously said the Guardian Angel prayer with me and my sister every night at bedtime. Not being Catholic, you may not know the Guardian Angel prayer," he assumed.

"I do not," Sherry confirmed. "Let's say I know about angels, but don't know anything about Guardian Angels."

Justin began, "Actually, it's a comforting notion as a kid. The idea is that a heavenly creature, an angel, a messenger, is assigned to protect and guide an individual from birth and throughout one's life. I still remember the prayer, 'Angel of God, my guardian dear, to whom God's love commits you here, ever this night (or day) be at my side to light and guard, to rule and guide. Amen.'

"Monique told me the other day on my birthday that the idea of a Guardian Angel is maybe another way to talk about Grace, or the Holy Spirit. Angels are in Hebrew scripture as well as Christian. Angels' wings maybe suggest action, activity, movement. In a secular sense, angels may be images of Infinite Creative Energy custom-made for us in our lifetime, to help us find our way, our path. These are Monique's ideas; I never know where my mom gets them."

Justin was in a good mood this evening, and why wouldn't he be? He'd made a lot of money on the real estate transaction. He survived another birthday and his mother's ostentatious fussing over his having been born on the Guardian Angels' Feast Day.

Plus, Justin was no longer burdened or perplexed by the huge amount of psychological material he and Sherry had gone over from Francine's folder. Either this psychological stuff settled someplace inside him or left his memory completely, except for one piece of information, which was still alive in his thoughts, "The fellow with the two first names."

Sherry knew, "That would be Williams James in his 1902 book on religious experience, and what he calls non-rational operations such as dreams, mystical experiences, intuitions, hypotheses, fancies, superstitions, persuasions, convictions, current inactive memories, everything unrecorded or unobserved, obscure passions, impulses, likes, dislikes, prejudices. Today, we might say these are activities of the right-hemisphere of the brain, the elder sibling because it forms first in the womb."

Justin concluded, "The first chunk of who we are."

"Seems so," Sherry agreed, "which may be labeled un-conscious, largely unknown to us, hidden from ourself; sometimes apparent to others. Francine sometimes talks about ego-me-I observations and awareness in contrast to this vast part of us we scarcely know, which is what Williams James was talking about. Sometimes I think ego-me-I is called mind, and the unknown part of us, soul. Mind and soul. Psyche means soul."

Sherry reflected aloud, "It is sometimes claimed we are powerfully, romantically attracted to another who mirrors back to us something about our own unknown psychological qualities; our own soul. We fall into attraction with someone who suggests (symbolically) something important about our life in a broad sense, not only our outer personality. Mostly, Francine finds romantic attraction and enduring love to be quite different."

"So it seems to me," Justin agreed cynically, "though I can't explain the difference. Romance often doesn't last."

Sherry continued, "Soul and mind aren't scientific concepts but more mythical ideas. However, just because they don't fit the scientific paradigm doesn't mean they're not real."

Justin stunningly remembered, "Which brings to mind, recently I was trolling on YouTube and came across a talk about Communion, the Eucharist, *transubstantiation*. I hadn't heard the word in years, maybe since I was preparing for my confirmation.

"Transubstantiation is about bread and wine being changed into the body and blood of Jesus. The bishop giving the talk made it clear transubstantiation is more profound than considering the bread and wine as symbol or metaphor. Transubstantiation isn't about appearance; transubstantiation is about essence."

Justin stopped short, "I know you're not Catholic."

Sherry replied, "Though I'm not Catholic, I've heard of transubstantiation from Francine. I'm acquainted with the meaning of the word. Maybe it's fairly accurate to say science is concerned with appearance, whereas myth is about essence. In that sense, Christianity is myth; the idea of transubstantiation is myth, but not in today's wrongly understood definition that myth means false, untrue. Myth exceeds physical reality, historical reality, commonsense reality. Myth at its purest is truth beyond all of these realities."

CHAPTER THIRTY-ONE

True Celibacy

Sherry extrapolated to herself about essence while stepping inside her apartment momentarily to retrieve another Francine folder. Sherry was thinking, *Marriage vows somehow change a relationship, clients have told me. It's not just the legality of the relationship that changes. Rather, the betweenness in the relationship, the essence of relationship itself is different because of words exchanged in a legal or religious setting.*

Sherry found the folder, *The ritual of the Mass*, and returned to the balcony.

Francine had written, "In Anglican/Episcopal, Catholic, and Eastern Christianity, the Eucharistic is the central sacramental, liturgical, celebration. This very old ritual involves both brain hemispheres, it seems to me."

> The goal of virtually every ritual ever performed [is] to lift participants out of their isolated individual sensibilities and immerse them in something larger than selves; the blending of the self into some larger reality (p. 80). . . religious rituals combine a mythic story with neurological reactions which bring the myth to

life (p. 95). . . the root of ceremonial rites is the neurobiological need to escape the limiting boundaries of the [left-hemisphere] self (p. 85)[20]

The purpose of ritual is to connect the present participants with the original event that the ritual commemorates and also to link them with all those who have participated in the ritual in the past. Ritual is something to do with crossing time, annihilating distance in time, bringing the past into the present. The Christian Holy Communion [Eucharist], for example, recreates or connects participants with the original Last Supper and also connects them with those who have participated since; it brings them into a connection with what is called the Communion of Saints.[21]

Francine wrote: "The word Eucharist means "thanksgiving." The Eucharist meal-ritual of The Last Supper is mystery in the sense of the Greek word <u>mysterion</u>. Our usual definition of mystery today does not express what Greek <u>mysterion</u> encapsulates. We might speak of a murder mystery, which is a story that needs to be solved; who committed the crime? Mystery in Greek is more than a puzzle, more than being puzzled or perplexed, more than simply an unanswered question.

"The Greek understanding of mystery pertains to revelation, wisdom, enlightenment about living and dying; the whole panorama of existence. In celebrating the Eucharist, the mystery of Jesus as paradigm-changing agent of the human condition exceeds human comprehension. <u>Mysterion</u> always exceeds human understanding. In Eucharist, the intuitive, holistic, emotional (right-hemisphere) functions commingle at the molecular level of embodied existence (our bodies) when consecrated bread and wine become part of our body and being. This incarnational ritual expresses thanks for what Jesus made available to humanity. Others have written about the mystery of the Eucharist."

---

[20] Andrew Newberg, Eugene D'Aquili, Vince Rause, *Why God Won't Go Away: Brain Science and the Biology of Belief,* (New York NY: Ballantine Books, 2001). See page numbers within quote above.

[21] Matthew Fox and Rupert Sheldrake, *Natural Grace: Dialogues on Creation, Darkness, and the Soul in Spirituality and Science,* (New York NY: Image Books, 1996), p. 166.

It commemorates and represents the Last Supper which our
Lord took with His disciples, the whole Incarnation, Passion,
Death and Resurrection of Christ. But from the point of view of
the divine, this anthropomorphic [human] action is only the
outer shell of husk in which what is really happening is not a
human action at all but a divine event.[22]

Brain science says humans experience "revelation" when both
sides of the brain are in agreement, creating "neurological resonance"(p. 72). Eucharist is an optimal occasion for neurological
resonance: whole-brain harmony, whole-brain agreement.
Church architecture, stained glass windows and other adorn-
ments, music, prayers, scripture readings, candles, incense, vest-
ments, gestures, heighten the five senses and alert the brain's
amygdala, that this a special place, a special happening. This psy-
cho-biological stimulation, when blended with silent calm, invites religious awe, (p. 89) and generates enchantment on a con-
tinuum from mild to intense.[23]

Francine added her own thoughts, "Eucharist is built on cognitive
underpinnings of the Jesus story, and the ritualistic atmosphere fosters
neurological resonance. To Christians who have Eucharist as their central
ritual, it is a psycho-spiritual Messianic banquet, a sacred celebration, a
union of God and human."

To this day in the Greek Orthodox Church and other Eastern
Orthodox Churches, the idea of deification is central, and the
Eucharist is still referred to in the ancient way as a *mysterion*,

---

[22] C. G. Jung, "Transformation Symbolism in the Mass," *Pagan and Christian Mysteries:
Papers from the Eranos Yearbooks,* translated by Ralph Manheim and R.F.C. Hull, edited
by Joseph Campbell, (New York NY: Harper & Row, 1955), p. 123.
[23] Andrew Newberg, Eugene D'Aquili, Vince Rause, *Why God Won't Go Away: Brain
Science and the Biology of Belief,* (New York NY: Ballantine Books, 2001). See page numbers
within quote above.

expressing the ineffable mystery of the union of Christ with the soul.[24]

Justin's thoughts seemed elsewhere. There was silence until Justin wanted to know, "As a psychotherapist, would you say most people come to therapy wanting to know what's on their mind, or what's in their soul?"

"Oh!" Sherry's face slightly scrunched, she fake-gasped. "Why don't you ask something difficult." She thought a moment and said, "People mostly want to stop hurting, to resolve something that is giving them emotional pain, behavioral or relationship problems, or all of this. Very often they come to therapy trying to figure out how to change someone else in their life.

"However, some people are eager, even desperate, to go deep into their psyche and uncover what might be hidden there. Others are afraid of doing that. The art of counseling is to correctly sense who wants to do what when, which is what is remarkably effective with the pamphlet Francine wrote on dreams where one can stand back from the dream and use metaphor with it, or go closer to the dream, and interact with aspects of the dream."

Justin had another question, "Do you find many people notice there might be a connection between brain-hemisphere preference and sexual attraction preference?" Sherry responded, I'm not sure I understand what you're asking."

Justin returned to Francine's mobius band, "I can see validity about gender differences in Francine's *yin-yang* lists, the possibility of gender identification between the lists, but I can't see same-sex sexual attraction related to the lists."

Sherry thoughtfully replied, "First, I think of the *yin-yang* lists as a mix of traditional (culturally-conditioned) and innate (genetic) tendencies. Whatever goes into the mix, it seems to me there is in everyday lived-life, masculine energy-essence and feminine energy-essence. And now you are asking about the dynamics which attract us to masculine or feminine essence-energy, is that correct?"

"I guess that's what I'm saying."

---

[24] John A. Sanford, *Mystical Christianity: A Psychological Commentary on the Gospel of John*, New York: Crossroad Publishing Co., 1993), p. 218.

"I have to say I don't have the answer to that, and I doubt anyone does. Some individuals perhaps come to understand this for themselves, however, I don't know of an overall answer that applies to everyone. Darwin's survival of the fittest doesn't seem to apply, for homosexuals tend not to reproduce, so the trait should disappear in the gene-pool, yet this has not happened."

Sherry continued on a slightly different note, "There's much we don't understand. How is it that people commit to celibate lives because of ideals, usually religious convictions, which seems unnatural, yet here are the words of an English anthropologist, "True celibacy far from being an affair of sexual repression, if rightly understood, is the most complete expression of the transformed sex instinct."[25] "Think of it, he says celibacy can be 'the most complete expression of the transformed sex instinct,'" as she pulled another paper from Francine's folder. "What is this anthropologist saying?"

Not waiting for an answer from herself or Justin, she read from another source.

> The neurological machinery of transcendence may have arisen from the neural circuitry that evolved for mating and sexual experience . . . the language of mysticism and sexual orgasm is much the same: bliss, rapture, ecstasy, exaltation. This does not mean, however, that they are the same experience. Neurologically, in fact, the two are quite different. Sexual bliss is primarily generated by the hypothalamus. Transcendent experiences depend upon the involvement of higher cognitive structures in the frontal lobe and other association areas. An evolutionary perspective suggests that the neurobiology of mystical experience arose, at least in part, from the mechanisms of the sexual response. In a sense then, mystical experience may be an accidental by-product, but this does not necessarily diminish the meaning of spiritual experience.[26]

---

[25] John Layard, "The Incest Taboo and the Virgin Archetype," *Eranos* 12, 1945, p. 286.
[26] Andrew Newberg, Eugene D'Aquili, Vince Rause, *Why God Won't Go Away: Brain Science & The Biology of Belief* (New York NY: Ballantine Books, 2001), pp. 125-126.

Sherry hoped she would someday build folders of her own as Francine had done over the years. She also realized Francine's quotes were mostly from male sources, and hoped her own stash would include more females.

She appreciated again that Francine was experienced enough to introduce religion into therapy at the right time, in the right way, if and when clients were open to the prospect. Sherry knew she still lacked what Francine had developed over time. Therefore, Sherry lived in conflict with herself, feeling she hid spiritual aspects of what she sometimes felt might have been most helpful for a client.

Sherry felt she gathered from her father and his ministry the tendency to lead with religion when psychology might sometimes have more to offer. She found as a therapist, personalities sometimes hide behind religion, reciting religious platitudes, having been conditioned in ways that distance them from being more authentically in touch with themselves, needing to learn new ways of being.

"Religion can be actually detrimental in these instances, until or unless the idea of the soul sets in. Once they know psyche means soul, and they relate the word soul to religion, they can begin to move towards their own inner world as a reality wanting, needing, longing to fill empty spots within, or shadow issues which need to be brought into the light of awareness through psychology (study of the soul) that is compatible with wisdom in the bible, religion, theology. I repeatedly realize that psychology without religion or religion without psychology—each lack what it might otherwise offer."

These days, Francine was seeing fewer clients, knowing the day would come when she no longer had the stamina for a full-time schedule, and her eyes, though reasonably stable at the moment, were always problematic. She continued to speak in-depth with Sherry about clients such as Kelly and Paul, who were especially motivated during the pandemic instability to make their marriage work. They agreed this would be the worst time ever to separate. Actually, neither wanted to end the marriage—but to improve it.

CHAPTER THIRTY-TWO

Altered States

Quinn and Bios ran to the Kendrick home almost daily where Cynthia and Pixie-Pickett then joined them on a walk in a nearby park. Cynthia and dog were outside waiting for Quinn and dog this exceptionally hot and humid day. After the walk in the park, Cynthia asked if he needed more ice in his water bottle and he agreed, lightheartedly teasing her about dealing with his water supply as she had the first day they met in the parking lot at the animal shelter. A few minutes later in the Kendrick kitchen he told Dee he had begun to read her commentary of Jesus' parables.

He mostly commented on the fourfold format she'd used, impressed with her approach, though he had little knowledge of the long history of allegorical exegesis. He casually made the observation that a multi-layered paradigm such as Dee applied might help today's culture overcome with too much singlemindedness in current politics, referring to Zach's napkin polarized drawing using the human eye. "Should a subtle, nuanced, multi-layered way of looking at life become a habit, then politics, citizens, culture, would surely benefit." Dee's four categories made sense to Quinn, which was the most feedback she'd received on her effort so far.

They talked about the day's walk in the park and then, about Brother Lawrence and his understanding about Nature, how trees changing from winter to spring was life-changing for the eighteen-year-old who became a monk. Quinn had told Cynthia he wasn't personally drawn to altered states of awareness, though many seem to want them.

When Quinn and Bios departed, Cynthia commented to Dee, "Quinn has said he isn't drawn to altered states of awareness, yet the whole reason for our walking in the park is for exactly that—to replenish, renew me, change the pitiful state I'm in. He's mentioned running and a "runner's high," associated with the release of endorphins. He is quite fond of running. I must mention his inconsistency to him. He may enjoy altered states more than he knows. He seems to count it a mark of sufficiency that his awareness of Enduring Presence in his life is all he wants or needs. Well, his awareness of Enduring Presence is perhaps reinforced by endorphins."

Dee agreed, "Altered states come in all sizes, mild to profound. Maybe it's satisfying to have such confidence as Quinn possesses. As for myself, I wish I could have a brain scan when I'm seeing purple to see what's going on in my brain." She remembered reading about a researcher doing brain scans on people in contemplative states saying there's a link between mystical experience and observable brain function, and the brain seems to have the built-in ability to transcend the perception of an individual self, a talent for self-transcendence which lies at the root of the religious urge.[27] And that humans are natural mystics blessed with an inborn genius for effortless self-transcendence.[28]

Dee could never dismiss her own experiences of dazzling, shimmering steadfast purple in what she would call episodes of contemplation. She didn't know if this was a brain activity, an eye event, or a combination of the two. She wondered how Jesus prayed. He said he was one with the Father. He had to have experienced intimacy which filled him with compassionate wisdom.

She remembered reading about mystical experience as wisdom. She went to her study and found her notebook of quotes. She found words

---

[27] Andrew Newberg, Eugene D'Aquili, Vince Rause, *Why God Won't Go Away: Brain Science & The Biology of Belief* (New York NY: Ballantine Books, 2001), p. 174.
[28] Andrew Newberg, *Why God Won't Go Away*, p. 113.

by the late William Johnston, an Irish Jesuit who lived in Japan for many years and was well acquainted with Asian mysticism. He equates mysticism with wisdom.

> By mysticism I mean wisdom. I mean the wisdom that goes beyond words and letters, beyond reasoning and thinking, beyond imaging and fantasy, beyond before and after into the timeless reality. There are flashes of mysticism in the life of anyone who prays . . . Mysticism, then, is quite different from the knowledge that comes from understanding and judging. Mystics of all religions will say that the wisdom I call mystical is not acquired by human effort. It is a gift that may come suddenly and unpredictably. Yet it can coexist with ordinary knowledge, and it does so after a new level of consciousness has been awakened in the human mind.[29]

The Jesuit also wrote of 'self-emptying,' a powerful common feature in both Asian meditation and Christian contemplation.

> This is the process of emptying oneself of attachment and clinging and grasping of any kind. One even lets go of imagining and thinking and reasoning. The process is one of total emptiness leading to total fullness.[30]

Total emptiness that leads to total fullness is quite different from nagging emptiness that leads that leads to fatigue, depression, a lackluster existence. Dee knew a thing or two about that. She found another comment she'd kept on mysticism.

> True mystical experiences are divine blessings that deepen compassion and give energy to the individual. They are transformatory points that help to sway a person's life from habitual egotism to selflessness . . . they require a spiritual commitment and

---

[29] William Johnston, *"Arise, My Love…": Mysticism for A New Era,* (Maryknoll NY: Orbis Books, 2000), p. xvi.
[30] William Johnston, *"Arise, My Love…"* p. 61.

discipline based on humility and faith . . . the result of contemplation is love, a love that makes no distinction between great and small, rich or poor, worthy or unworthy . . . The mystics teach us how to reach God not through clouds of joy and ecstasy and angelic choirs but through the deepening of love.[31]

Dee thought about the wisdom in Quinn's suggestion that a daily walk in nature could replenish Cynthia, and realized also the loving action in Quinn's offer to come by with Bios and walk with Cynthia and Pixie-Pickett, whose everyday name was often Pix or Picks. A walk fostered a change of scenery, temporarily removing Cynthia from the stress of trying to distance-teach very young students. He knew the challenge of being a first-year teacher. He'd done that, but under conditions far better than now with the pandemic, and he could empathize with Cynthia.

Dee hoped Cynthia would not attack Quinn in his inconsistency about himself, feeling he didn't need mysticism for he had ongoing caring Presence in his life, but not counting ongoing Presence as a kind of generalized mysticism. Not everyone experiences such. Surely Quinn knows that, Dee theorized.

Dee further felt Cynthia might not properly evaluate Quinn's concern for Cynthia. These days overall, Cynthia was becoming easier to live with, as if the trials of teaching were molding her into a better version of herself; not so high and mighty as she used to be. The change in Cynthia might also partially be Quinn himself.

One evening, Cynthia drove to Sherry's apartment and took with her, at Dee's suggestion, a copy of Dee's explication on Jesus' parables for Sherry. Dee still wanted feedback from someone other than Zach, who found what she'd done renewing, which he related to profoundly, easily.

Cynthia and Sherry watched the 2011 movie *Hugo*, at Sherry's apartment.

---

[31] James Harpur, *Love Burning in the Soul: The Story of the Christian Mystics, from Saint Paul to Thomas Merton,* (Boston MA: New Seeds Books, 2005), p. 220.

CHAPTER THIRTY-THREE

The Movie, *Hugo*

Neither Sherry or Cynthia had seen the movie *Hugo*, yet wanted to. Afterwards, they talked about the first part of the movie, a fable beautifully tied to the second-half, a semi-documentary about French illusionist and motion picture pioneer, Georges Melies (1861-1938), whose films of fantasy, at first hugely popular, lost favor against the horrors of World War I, bringing eventual financial ruin to Melies, and then he faded into obscurity.

Sherry and Cynthia psychologically interpreted the magical story of 12-year-old Hugo, an orphan, living with his drunken uncle, who maintains clocks in a train station in Paris after World War I, while living in an apartment in the clock tower. Hugo stays in the apartment and keeps the station's clocks working after his uncle disappears and his body is sometime later found in the Seine River.

Cynthia and Sherry decided everyone is to a degree a psychological orphan, feeling somewhat alone in the world, aching to be filled with hope; meaningful purpose, caring Presence. They theorized that to temper this psychological orphan aspect, in Judeo-Christianity there is God as Father. In Catholic and Orthodox Christianity there is also Mary as Mother.

Sherry and Cynthia looked at the movie as everybody's psychological story working itself out over TIME. We are, like Hugo, orphans living a Time-ruled existence (clocks and trains run on time) and in a sense as we mature, we have schedules, must make things happen in a Timely way with calendars, appointments, until it is Time for us to die. Until death, we live, metaphorically speaking, in a train station, traveling through life largely in the way we have been trained, conditioned, learned to be, following certain tracks, patterns, pathways, habits.

Thus, our station in life includes to one degree or another, an aspect of our personality that finds Time Itself harsh, unrelenting, punishing, portrayed as the station inspector with his fierce dog in the movie.

Orphan Hugo was given a robot (a built-to-write automaton) by his father just as ancestry, parents, environment are "givens" for all of us. The robot has a keyhole the shape of a heart, but the key to the heart, which would bring the robot alive, is lost. Likewise, we must find the key to who we are most naturally, our unique contribution, our heart's desire, our purpose, just as Hugo was concerned with "purpose." He said machines have a purpose—they do what they are meant to do. Broken machines made him sad; he wanted to fix them because they were unable to do what they were intended to do. People can also be broken, unable to do what they are invited by the cosmos to do.

Hugo meets 12-year-old Isabelle, also an orphan who, astonishingly, wears the heart-shaped key which they need to activate the automaton which does not write, but instead draws a unique image of the moon; of great significance in the movie.

And aren't we all looking for the key to having a psychological picture of doing what makes us come alive! Part of the key to life is learning to value and use both hemispheres of our brain, Sherry and Cynthia agreed, laughing at how unavoidable that conclusion would be for them under the influence of Francine and Dee.

The meeting of Hugo and Isabelle, Cynthia and Sherry likened to brain hemispheres which together produce the key to life: commonsense compassionate wisdom bringing forth a Time of practical well-being for everyone, probably like Jesus' Kingdom of God, Sherry suggested.

The friendship of Hugo and Isabelle might depict the mix of feminine and masculine energy in each person which brings forth heart, real heart that unlocks the value of images such as sleeptime dreams. Sherry took notice that the automaton drew an image rather than writing the alphabet, words.

She remembered the brain's left-hemisphere language areas, whereas the right-hemisphere produces images. She recalled laparoscopic surgeon Shlain writing in his 1998 book, The *Alphabet Versus The Goddess: The Conflict Between Word and Image,* that culture's left-hemisphere alphabet literacy preference is today correcting itself because of images, the pictures from television, videos, and movies. Shlain also said two-hand typing instead of one-hand writing has brought brain preference changes. The computer "mouse" causes hand-eye coordination which is more spatial than linear, and invites right-brain pattern skills.

In the movie, a train crashes through the train station, not unlike psychologically feeling explosive, or having crashed emotionally because of the demands and constraints of Time. Or on occasion, moments, minutes, episodes of explosive insights, synchronicities, out-of-the-ordinary happenings. Hugo perilously hangs outside onto a clock hand in the clock tower, to keep from tragically falling. We know what it's like to barely hang-on when Time and sheer survival seem to demand so much of us. At other Times, it is quite lovely to lose track of Time during enjoyment.

So, is Time a blessing or a curse? Both, of course. Is mysticism a break of Timelessness into Time, a peek past Time, a meeting of Time and Timelessness? All of these, perhaps.

The daughter of a pastor, Sherry wondered whether human sin is entirely responsible for making life askew. What about the heaviness, the challenges of Time Itself? Does Time come from Sin? Or does Sin come from Time? Likely, the two are not connected, and yet they are. And isn't Time also a gift?

Time from the rotation of the earth, day-night, moon cycles, changing seasons. Planet earth rotates and creates Time. Time is a neutral 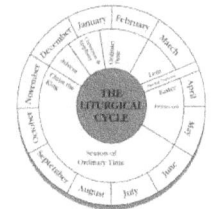 agent? It's what earthlings do with Time that makes a difference: Our choices. Our decisions. Our interpretations. Cynthia remembered Dee speaking of the liturgical calendar, which blends the Christ saga with seasons of the year, a mythical interpretation of historical Jesus, whereby his story is tied to the cycle of seasons. "As the world turns," Cynthia grinned, using the title of an old TV soap opera. Then, acting as if pulling out her hair, "I must not use the I-word, *interpretation*, or the H-word, *hermeneutics*," Cynthia laughed, "That's Dee's passion."

And then Cynthia was serious, "I have come to realize the death of my biological mother has kept me from embracing religion. Since I was young, I've not been interested in anything that let my mother die. I still carry this within me, which has fueled my difficulty with Dee. I see this ever clearer in myself, as I know I suffer an emptiness that aches to be filled, though I feel I am meant to be a teacher, just not under Covid circumstances, and yet Covid is today's reality, therefore my reality." Cynthia's thoughts were scrambled yet poignant.

The evening with Sherry ended. Cynthia stepped outside to drive home, and was moonstruck, for a full moon that night shone on even the shadows of the night, and beckoned to something deep inside her. As the automaton in the movie drew an image of the moon that tied the film together, so too, Cynthia gazed at length at the moon and yearned to unite.

She ached to unite with nothing (no-thing) she could name, which was more real than words. Yet, a word came: INFINITY. Cynthia slowly drove home in the moonlit glow, with the word INFINITY in mind and then, surprisingly caring for the first time what Dee created with Jesus' parables. Why was Cynthia now interested in Dee's work?

Cynthia realized influences had come together in her this evening. In *Hugo* the automaton's moon drawing was signed with an elaborate swirl-enhanced infinity sign, and the word infinity later came to her connected to the full moon shining in this night. Then, there had been Sherry's mention of Jesus' Kingdom of God, plus Cynthia had given a copy of Dee's work on Jesus' parables to Sherry, and the parables are stories about the Kingdom of God or heaven, so Dee's work was on Cynthia's mind in some way.

Thus, the word Infinity and Dee's work had converged, along with the synchronicity of the moon's importance in the movie and the full moon shining in the nighttime sky, when Cynthia stepped outside. All together, these happenings brought forth curiosity in Cynthia to read Dee's completed parables project.

Cynthia knew enough about dreams through Francine and Dee to know that dreams tend to be highly associative, linking this-to-that and much more. She concluded that her desire to read Dee's work on the parables rose out of threads woven together into a pattern of importance this evening with Sherry.

Once home, Cynthia flipped through her copy of Dee's completed project, which she would begin to read tomorrow, or so she told herself.

CHAPTER THIRTY-FOUR

Grandson Dexter

Happily for Dee, sidewalk professor Oriana now living in New York telephoned to talk about the completed parables project she'd received from Dee and read carefully.

Oriana found in Dee's explication and extrapolation of Jesus' parables an echo of American philosopher-psychologist Ken Wilber's writing about "three eyes," three ways of attaining knowledge: flesh, mind, and contemplation used by St. Bonaventure who knew that earthly existence requires looking at life in different ways, seeking different kinds of truth. Religion does not give scientific answers. Science does not provide religious, mythical truths. We must recognize different realms or layers of reality. Bonaventure used three categories while the old exegesis had four categories. Surely, the *moral* category was assumed in Bonaventure's mindset; however, his task was one of epistemology (how we come to know) rather than hermeneutics (how we interpret).

Oriana complimented the boldness of Dee to revamp old allegorical exegesis for use today. And she mentioned the wisdom in Dee demonstrating the physical-material-sense interpretation of Jesus' stories to show the constricted rigidity and inadequacy of so-called strict literalism.

Oriana was hopeful as a culture we are outgrowing constricted ways of understanding. She observed, "To do science, it is necessary to control variables—extraneous issues which clutter what is under investigation. The human mind can only deal with so many things at one time, so humans learned how to reduce variables. However, now with computers that can process many variables at one time, more and more variables can be pumped-into a situation. We are in a state of expansion rather than reduction when looking at situations.

"In ordinary, everyday life we do not get to throw out variables, every aspect of a situation is part of the reality we experience. Therefore, we need right-hemisphere whole-view insights, perspectives, to accompany partial but important bits of information along the way."

Oriana effusively told Dee, "I find it lovely you honor your aunt re-thinking the parables out of your own experience, which makes clear the personal context in which you are relating to the stories. You are not writing with a cultural-historical view from the time Jesus was on earth, or from traditional or theological points of view.

"Further, it seems to me a stroke of uncommon insight that you took abandoned allegorical exegesis and reframed it for use today, which might encourage others to update tradition when and where possible. You emphasize soul, psyche, deep personality with rich, varied vocabulary, giving an informed voice to vital human experience—what passes through our being.

"I so appreciate that at Eucharist we declare, 'Only say the word and my SOUL shall be healed,' the importance of soul-healing; deep calling to deep. I believe humanity longs to belong to what is Ultimate. Longing is nostalgia, in Greek, *nostos* 'to return home,' *algos* 'pain.' In German, *das Sehnen,* 'connected to something distant, separated, removed from.'"

Oriana spoke of her deceased husband, "In his last days he repeatedly said he wanted to go 'home.' When I asked him if that meant Puerto Rico, he said 'no.' I'd mention this house or that house he'd lived in, but he always said 'no.' I came to feel it was a psychological or spiritual place for which he yearned, he longed; an existential ache. Perhaps the craving one has for mood-changing drugs to go to a 'home' place inside, in the soul, that ancient word which can't be exactly defined or located. An idea beyond precise meaning.

Oriana continued, "It seems to me the parables overall tend to coalesce into Jesus' words, 'Forgive our trespasses as we forgive those who trespass against us,' and 'Love your neighbor as yourself,' for if one is out of touch with oneself, that person will have limited understanding of others as well—ending with a lack of psychological wisdom about oneself and others.

"To me, your metaphoric articulations of the parables bring the hope of subtlety and nuance. Perhaps culture can evolve into greater justice, mercy and hope should metaphoric discernment become widespread when applied to oneself. I greatly appreciate what you've explicated and extrapolated." This was the gist of what Oriana said to Dee on the telephone, and Dee was filled with joyful gratitude.

Meanwhile, Estelle's Grandson, Dexter, unexpectedly came to live with her. Now that students were doing online classes at home because of Covid, he and his parents increasingly clashed, which was their usual way of relating. His father had always been absent a good bit, working on oil rigs in the Gulf of Mexico. His mother tried to be both mother and father, which Dexter could not bear, and his disrespect increased as her controlling tactics multiplied with his age.

One day, while his dad was on an oil rig, after another confrontation with his mother, Dexter packed his car and told his mother he was going to grandmother Estelle's. On the drive there, Dexter telephoned his grandmother to tell her he was on the way, and gave a short version of the circumstances.

Estelle was perplexed, overwhelmed, yet not surprised. She waited for him in a state of anxiety. Dexter was in a buoyant mood when he arrived. The two talked for hours. Estelle listened and understood Dexter's assessment of his parents.

Dexter jested there was a mix-up in the hospital where he was born and he was sent home with the wrong parents. Estelle suggested he might be of a different temperament type than either of his parents. She knew also that the family had moved a number of times because of his dad's job and changing schools and friends was not easy for Dexter. He resented always being the new kid at school, leaving friends, again and again.

"My parents don't talk about what I care about. They're good parents in many ways but they don't ask big questions about life. If I try and talk about what I want to do in the future, my parents claim I don't know what I'm talking about; I'm unrealistic. My mom argues with me, and my dad pokes fun of my ideas, wise-cracking put-downs like maybe they do to each other on oil rigs—tough smart-aleck crap that me and my guy friends do. But I don't want that from my parents. I want them to listen to me without always evaluating me, trying to make me be realistic, as they say.

Dexter continued, "I'm disrespectful to both my parents. They don't respect what I say, my ideas, and I don't respect them. They know I use psychedelics. Sometimes what the psychedelics do scares me, but other times I have beautiful experiences. My parents should try psychedelics to expand themselves, their small-minded concerns, boring, boring. If I try and introduce them to bigger ideas, that's when they start ripping at me."

Estelle had read about and seen videos on psychedelics after Dexter first told her he'd taken LSD. She was not totally unaware of teenage use of psychedelics when she was a school counselor, but Dexter made her super-concerned. She knew psychedelic usage was fairly commonplace with teenagers. She also knew there was renewed interest in treating mental/emotional illness with psychedelics. She was aware that psychedelics could provide chemically manipulated visions sometimes likened to spiritual visions.

Estelle questioned within herself, not for the first time, *Why don't seekers envision the gospel stories as is done in the Spiritual Exercises of St. Ignatius of Loyola, or cherish their sleeptime visions, their dreams. These vision experiences happen without ingesting chemicals. She might talk with Dexter about this, if it seems appropriate.*

Dexter was raised without religion. Estelle's son Ross, Dexter's father, grew up Catholic. His wife Shannon's family went to an evangelical church. Both Ross and Shannon gave up church upon marrying, not wanting religion to be an issue in the marriage. Estelle was aware that many in the U.S. stopped going to church in recent years.

Estelle didn't know how long Dexter would be with her. She knew he'd be working on school assignments online as class attendance at his high school was cancelled due to the Covid epidemic, which might be why he'd risked leaving home at this time. He did want to graduate with his class. She wondered how long it would take for him to find living with his grandmother boring; how long before he'd miss being with his friends rather than being in touch with them at a distance.

He talked with Estelle about his friends and how they did and did not get along with their parents. Who did and did not use psychedelics and what he thought about that. He summarized, "We all sorta have an empty something inside us. Some, more than others." Estelle saw in Dexter great sensitivity, an insightfulness she'd seen in him even when he was very young.

Estelle and Dexter talked a great deal those first few days; they clearly respected each other. Dexter noticed Dee's work on the parables of Jesus in a plastic binder on the arm of Estelle's recliner and asked her about it. Estelle told him about her friend Dee and the contents of the binder.

Several days later during a meal, he said he'd read a little in the binder, and summarized, "It's an easy read; one story at a time plus your friend's comments on the story aren't long, so that's doable." Estelle was amused by his primary concern with brevity.

Dexter continued, "I think it's amazing of your friend to do this for her dead aunt. I've only read a little bit, but so far, I like it. I like how your friend divides everything into four short categories, and talks about personality." Estelle had not before thought that Dee's format might appeal to adolescents for its brevity and psychological content.

Dexter's comment about his friends having an "empty something" reminded Estelle of Reggie's desire to "go home" in his final weeks, reinforced by Dee's friend Oriana's husband's desire to "go home" before his death, which Oriana referred to as an "existential ache." We do, all of us, have an aching soul, which Estelle found Dee's extrapolation of Jesus' parables overall speaks to.

After three weeks with his grandmother, Dexter drove back to living with his family. Estelle sent a copy of Dee's explications of Jesus' parables with him, and she herself reread the binder with the eyes of a teenager, or at least that was her intention, which seemed to lessen her anxiety about Dexter and his family, though she was certain a teenager has not lived long enough to grasp the fullness of experience embodied in Dee's rendition of the parables.

However, Estelle may have underestimated the impact of Dee's work on Dexter, who told his grandmother he occasionally read a parable and Dee's fourfold explication. Amazingly, Dexter was eventually able to say he had insights about himself. He realized how much fear was in him because he grew-up afraid his dad would be injured or killed in his dangerous work on oil rigs. The absence of his father made it seem as if his father was already gone forever; as if the worst had already happened. And he resented his mother trying to play the role of his absent father; having to be tough through the years. And having to move too often also made him fearful about never belonging—starting over again and again, which he now understood caused him to accumulate more fear and anger. He said maybe he understood this about himself because Dee's work with the parables loosened him up enough to realize something about his fear and anger.

Estelle could not stop being grateful for Dee's extrapolations. She found profound her dear friend's bold return to exponential understanding in old fourfold exegesis adapted to today's world.

CHAPTER THIRTY-FIVE

Jesus' Parables

Fourfold Understanding
of
Jesus' Parables
by
Dee Kendrick
in loving memory of Aunt Teresa (Tess)

Introduction

I wish my aunt and I had had conversations about Jesus' parables, but I didn't know about fourfold interpretation of the bible uncovered by Gabby and Matti, until I read material from Matti's computer. I learned hermeneutics is the study of interpretation, and that in Christianity interpreting the Bible in four ways (literal, allegorical, moral, spiritual) was standard practice for more than a thousand years.

I began this project in memory of aunt Teresa who said Jesus' parables often did not make much sense to her. Having felt that way myself in times past, I share below my understanding of what Jesus' parables have come to mean to me.

I present Jesus' parables using a modified, revised, updated fourfold format:

1. Outer-world: five-sense physical-material exterior experience
2. Inner-world: interior experience of soul, psyche, deep personality
3. Making choices: morality, ethics, human choices and their consequences
4. Spiritually: the Kingdom of God which Jesus embodied and talked about

I begin with the parable of the wooden plank in one's eye. Thank you, aunt Teresa, for being patient with the planks in my personality. Jesus is shown to repeatedly say his stories are about the reign of God or heaven on earth. I feel certain the world gets better one personality at a time. Therefore, I may seem to over-emphasize individual psyche, soul, deep personality.

I look at our world which needs more justice, mercy, sharing the tangible and intangible *goods* of earth, where too often personalities inflict onto others, approaches to life that are unwholesome, even destructive. I therefore highlight the challenges and creative hope of deep personality, soul, psyche, in Jesus' parables. My comments are metaphoric, symbolic, fourfold, as was old, allegorical exegesis.

-1-

Splinter and Wooden Beam in Eyes

Why do you notice the splinter in your brother's eye, but do not perceive the wooden beam in your own? How can you say to you brother, 'Brother, let me remove that splinter in your eye,' when you do not even notice the wooden beam in your own eye? You hypocrite! Remove the wooden beam from your eye first; then you will see clearly to remove the splinter in your brother's eye. (Luke 6:41-42)

Outer-world:

Two people each have a foreign object in their eye, which needs removal. These are practical instructions similar to flight instructions on an airplane to put your own oxygen supply on first before helping someone else attach their oxygen supply.

Inner-world:

The lesson is about the importance of self-knowledge, self-awareness; coming to know the unknown in one's own personality, which includes unlived potential, as well as shortcomings, limitations, incompleteness, and old psychological wounds which push and pull within. We all have such.

Making choices:

Daily life demands we "size-up" others. Trying not to notice obstacles in others is a kind of dishonesty. Yet, how ethical is it for me to notice others' flaws with my own shortcomings blurring my psychological vision? The answer: increasing self-discernment brings more compassionate discernment about others. (Love your neighbor as yourself).

My primary human task is getting to know the limitations and potential in my own personality, which is a much richer way of including what was perhaps intended in an "examination of conscience," invaluable morally, though insufficient psychologically.

Spiritually:

Jesus, Mary, and Joseph were unusual humans. To the followers of the wise, shamanic, holy man Jesus, he was the long-awaited Messiah. Mary spoke with an angel about her pregnancy. Joseph saved the lives of Mary and Jesus by paying attention to his dreams. These three humans were "divinized" (filled with grace) in different ways to different degrees.

Jesus came to be known as fully human and fully divine. Humanity needs and wants to be touched by what is divine. We seek It while It seeks us. There are personal splinters and wooden beams which need to be dealt with in each personality.

-2-

Lamp on a Stand

No one who lights a lamp conceals it with a vessel or sets it under a bed; rather, he places it on a lampstand so that those who enter may see the light. For there is nothing hidden that will not become

visible, and nothing secret that will not be known and come to light. Take care, then, how you hear. To anyone who has, more will be given, and from the ones who has not, even what he seems to have will be taken away. (Luke 8:16-18)

Outer-world:

Most of this parable is a commonsense statement of the obvious: one doesn't turn on a light and then prevent it from shining in the area it is capable of lighting. To stunt or conceal the light's capacity is a waste of lamp oil (or electricity). This parable is a both a comment against being wasteful with light sources, as well as the consequences of being a poor listener.

Inner-world

Though this parable is about light, and not splinters and wooden beams, the theme is essentially the same: seek personal enlightenment, insight. I have come to value paying attention to dreams and now also contemplative praying, or any kind of deep prayer "from the gut," our depths. This requires being psychologically open to the constant lessons Life is teaching us about our personality, whether pleasant or unpleasant.

There seems to be another lesson in this parable about not allowing one's self-knowledge to be ignored, frittered away, lessened by others, or acquiescing to a less enlightened frame of reference. Compromising one's own knowing erodes integrity, leads to feeling compromised, disquieted, upset, ill-at-ease, at odds with oneself. The word integrity comes from the Latin integer, *which means whole or unbroken. Violating one's own integrity brings feelings of being fragmented; scattered within.*

Making choices:

How does one learn to listen well? Conscience is traditionally the word summing up personality's barometer which registers rightness or wrongness. Conscience is an "inner light" which can be extinguished through neglect, being tossed aside, leaving one in the dark without a moral compass to safeguard one's well-being and the well-being of others.

Conscience is not only about good or bad behavior, it's also about ignoring, not defending, minimizing commonsense wisdom within the personality; leaving darkened understanding, an individual less able to make wise decisions. Listen, pay attention to feelings, to bodily symptoms — to what they might be "saying."

<u>Spiritually:</u>
The parable says everything hidden and secret will become known. There are two kinds of light: one is the opposite of heavy, and the other the opposite of dark. Daily living becomes less heavy as we more and more "see" our own psychological stumbling blocks—and unique giftedness.

Those who have will be given more and those who only seem to have will lose even that, implies people who seek self-knowledge (both what is pleasant and unpleasant) will no longer be in the dark about themselves, become less fragmented, more whole and comfortable in their own skin. While those with little self-knowledge may find their journey, their personality, increasingly scattered and burdensome.

-3-
The Lost Sheep & the Lost Coin

What man among you having a hundred sheep and losing one of them would not leave the ninety-nine in the desert and go after the lost one until he finds it? And when he does find it, he sets it on his shoulders with great joy and, upon his arrival home, he calls together his friends and neighbors and says to them, 'Rejoice with me because I have found my lost sheep.' I tell you, in just the same way there will be more joy in heaven over one sinner who repents than over ninety-nine righteous people who have no need of repentance. (Luke 15:4-7)

Or what woman having ten coins and losing one would not light a lamp and sweep the house, searching carefully until she finds it? And when she does find it, she calls together her friends and neighbors and says to them, 'Rejoice with me because I have found the coin that I lost.' In just the same way, I tell you, there will be rejoicing among the angels of God over one sinner who repents. (Luke 15:8-10)

<u>Outer-world:</u>
Losing earthly objects like sheep or coins is upsetting to humans. Finding the objects brings joy. In this story God is said to be like a human, upset when humans themselves become lost and need to be found. The word "repent" is key to the dilemma.

Inner-world:

One may feel lost, lose hope, lose interest in being alive, lose courage, feel bewildered, alone, not knowing where to go in the inner or outer world to find a way out of being lost in desperation, hopelessness, depression, fear. The priority in these two stories is recovering what has been lost. Psychologically speaking, this means restoring traits, qualities, facets of personality, to their healthy, life-enhancing potential.

Recovery depends on one's willingness to be open to God's grace. Repentance is the human act of saying "yes" to God's help. Salvation is another word, which in its fullest sense, includes healing, being salvaged, having "salve" put on our psychological wounds and the psychological wounds of others.

Making choices:

Though we may lose our way one tiny decision, dilemma, conundrum, puzzlement, quandary, quagmire, choice and consequence at a time, this is not our whole story. In the messiness of life, we are not always the sinner; we can also be sinned against, not just by others but by conditions, situations beyond our control. Sin, meaning "missing the mark" is simply part of earthly existence. Repentance is sincere contrition, acknowledging appropriate wrongness, and is the door which opens to atonement, at-one-ment, *reconciliation with oneself, others, God.*

Spiritually:

Compassionate Christ knows the ins and outs of human existence. He understands the core dynamics in psychological pain as well as the consequences of obstinate, hurtful human decisions. Jesus' parables of the lost and found tell us that Divine Love never stops seeking relationship with us, caring about our welfare, and rejoicing in us. We are never so lost that we cannot, in Divine love, find healing and meaning in being alive.

-4-

The Prodigal Son

A man had two sons, and the younger son said to his father, 'Father, give me the share of your estate that should come to me.' So the father divided the property between them. After a few days, the younger son collected all his belongings and set off to a distant country where he squandered his inheritance on a life of dissipation. When he had freely spent everything, a severe famine struck that country, and he found himself in dire need. So he hired himself out to one of the local citizens who sent him to his farm to tend the swine. And he longed to eat his fill of the pods on which the swine fed, but nobody gave him any. Coming to his senses he thought, 'How many of my father's hired workers have more than enough food to eat, but here am I, dying from hunger. I shall get up and go to my father and I shall say to him, "Father, I have sinned against heaven and against you. I no longer deserve to be called your son; treat me as you would treat one of your hired workers." So he got up and went back to his father. While he was still a long way off, his father caught sight of him, and was filled with compassion. He ran to his son, embraced him and kissed him. His son said to him, 'Father, I have sinned against heaven and against you; I no longer deserve to be called your son.' But his father ordered his servants, 'Quickly bring the finest robe and put it on him; put a ring on his finger and sandals on his feet. Take the fatted calf and slaughter it. Then let us celebrate with a feast, because this son of mine was dead, and has come to life again' he was lost, and has been found.' Then the celebration began. Now the older son had been out in the field and, on his way back, as he neared the house, he heard the sound of music and dancing. He called one of the servants and asked what this might mean. The servant said to him, 'Your brother has returned and your father has slaughtered the fattened calf because he has him back safe and sound.' He became angry, and when he refused to enter the house, his father came out and pleaded with him. He said to his father in reply, 'Look, all these years I served you and not once did I disobey your orders; yet you never gave me even a young goat to feast on with my friends. But when your son returns who swallowed up your property with prostitutes, for him you slaughter the fattened calf.' He said to him, 'My son, you are here with me always; everything I have is yours. But now we must celebrate and rejoice, because your brother was dead and has come to life again; he was lost and has been found.'" (Luke 15:11-32)

Outer-world:

The story warns against leaving one's familiar geographic area. Stay home as the complaining older son does in the story. Don't risk leaving.

Inner-world:

Being "at home" with oneself, as Jesus must have been when he healed on the Sabbath breaking a religious rule and getting himself into trouble, and when as an adolescent he was in the temple instead of "on the way home" with his parents. Do we know when we are and are not "at home" with the core of our being?

Making choices:

The younger son chose to leave home, and met failure, humiliation. The older son chose to stay home, safe but complaining, feeling cheated. Who learned more? Who was more morally honest, truer to himself?

Spiritually:

The parable twice tells us the lost has been found. Being "at home" with ever-loving Spirit, even if we've moved away from this font of grace at times, is cause for celebration personally and cosmically, in the universe at large.

-5-
Ten Gold Coins

A nobleman went off to a distant country to obtain the kingship for himself and then to return. He called ten of his servants and gave them ten gold coins and told them, 'Engage in trade with these until I return.' His fellow citizens, however, despised him and sent a delegation after him to announce, 'We do not want this man to be our king.' But when he returned after obtaining the kingship, he had the servants called, to whom he had given the money, to learn what they had gained by trading. The first came forward and said, 'Sir, your gold coin has earned ten additional ones.' He replied, 'Well done, good servant! You have been faithful in this very small Zacher; take charge of ten cities.' Then the second came and reported, 'Your gold coin, sir, has earned five more.' And to this servant too he said, 'You, take charge of five cities.' Then the other servant came and said, 'Sir, here is your gold coin; I kept it stored away in a handkerchief, for I was afraid of you, because you are a demanding person; you take up what you did not lay down and you harvest what you did not plant.' He said to him, 'With your own words I shall condemn you, you wicked servant. You knew I was a demanding person, taking up what I did not lay down and harvesting what I did not plant; why did you not put my money in a bank? Then on my return I would have collected it with interest.' And to those standing by he said, 'Take the gold coin from him and give it to the servant who has ten.' But they said to him, 'Sir, he has ten gold coins.' I tell you, to everyone who has, more will be given, but from the one who has not, even what he has will be taken away. Now as for those enemies of mine who did not want me as their king, bring them here and slay them before me." (Luke 19:12-27)

Outer-world:

The story is about using money to make money and how wrong it is to not do this. The nobleman is not noble, but harsh, even ordering murder. Citizens of his country rightly do not want him to be king because he is cruel.

Inner-world:

We are all in servitude to what it takes daily to survive and thrive. It takes noble effort to not be overwhelmed by chores and duties which being alive requires. For example, cleanliness and personal hygiene, brushing teeth, bathing, getting enough sleep, eating well, balancing work and play require wisdom and effort. Daily life can feel like a harsh taskmaster. Those with self-discipline fare better than those who hide from responsibility. Making little or no investment in what life asks of us, we get little or less in return. Dread, procrastination, guilt can slay our best intentions to respond to practical tasks of living.

Making choices:

The tiny, tiny choices we make daily add up to the investment we make in life and living, and whether or not we get a rich return. The inability to make ourselves do what we need to do increasingly compromises the Will; eventually causing a paralysis of Will.

<u>Spiritually:</u>
Having a malleable, pliable, adaptable attitude to what daily life demands from us is no small matter. Ordinary tasks can be harsh and cruelly demanding if attempted by human effort alone without the cosmic companionship which Jesus embodies and shares with us.

-6-
Garments & Wineskins

No one tears a piece from a new cloak to patch an old one. Otherwise, he will tear the new and the piece from it will not match the old cloak. Likewise, no one pours new wine into old wineskins. Otherwise, the new wine will burst the skins, and it will be spilled, and the skins will be ruined. Rather, new wine must be poured into fresh wineskins. [And] no one who has been drinking old wine desires new, for he says, "The old is good." (Luke: 5:36–39)

<u>Outer-world:</u>
This is practical information about patching clothes and making wine.

<u>Inner-world:</u>
Just as wine ferments, personality perspectives change over time. Some aspects are stretched, while others shrink. If inflexible, the personality may feel it will burst learning new lessons about itself. Each personality must patch up tears in its own mental and emotional world and have an elixir of hope to enjoy being alive. Shrinking and stretching are how the personality transforms. What is new is not always comfortable. Sometimes old approaches to life have their own comforts. Personality growth is a patchwork of experiences. The healthy personality is a vessel of change ready for ongoing creative development.

<u>Making choices:</u>
The only thing that does not change is change. One can embrace, resist, or grudgingly accept the rips and tears of life. Every personality needs repair and healing. We may shrink back from this truth or embrace it. Change as endless flux is unavoidable. Reaction to change has huge consequences for self and others. Technological change today happens at such a fast pace, one urgently needs something to hold onto.

Spiritually:

Jesus the Christ is humanity's elixir. In him, through him, with him, one's outer garment (exterior personality) as well as inner and inmost states evolve, sometimes through agitation and turmoil, altering one's state of consciousness, relations with others and with one's own deep being. In this parable Jesus may be alluding to conundrums encountered in his new disciples as they mix new and old ideas, paradigms, cultural and spiritual changes because of him. Jesus was and is a change-maker. He cushions the shock of change in our lives.

-7-

Mustard Seeds

What is the kingdom of God like? To what can I compare it? It is like a mustard seed that a person took and planted in the garden. When it was fully grown, it became a large bush and "the birds of the sky dwelt in its branches." (Luke 13:18-19)

If you have faith the size of a mustard seed, you would say to [this] mulberry tree, "Be uprooted and planted in the sea," and it would obey you. (Luke: 17:6)

Outer-world:

Twice, in the gospel of Luke, Jesus uses the tiny mustard seed to make a point to his farming audience.

Inner-world:

Desire for Being Itself may be tiny and overlooked, unnoticed amongst other drives, needs, and wants in the personality. However, once recognized this longing and yearning for ultimate, enduring fulfillment is realized as immense; a fundamental craving for contact with what is vital beyond all else; the source of life itself; an innate existential ache. Longing and yearning for Ultimate Reality is embedded in the human personality.

Ancestral and cultural inheritance is sometimes the seed which needs loving attention and healing, so that the height and depth of personality potential can be reached. Just as tiny mustard seeds embody amazing potential, so too, tiny inklings within the personality contain important implications and answers to daily life and living.

<u>Making choices:</u>

Does the religious impulse germinate best in (1) religious tradition, (2) common sharing, (3) individual spiritual experience? Likely, the best answer is all three are needed just as seeds need proper soil and sufficient sunlight and suitable water.

<u>Spiritually:</u>

Jesus the anointed one, the Christ, is the seed planted in the historical human story, in the soil of human struggle, in the toil of increasing human consciousness in the human soul (psyche). Small beginnings grow into large becomings in the personality, helping bring the kingdom of God to earth, one person at a time.

-8-
Seed Grows of Itself

This is how it is with the kingdom of God; it is as if a man were to scatter seed on the land and would sleep and rise night and day and the seed would sprout and grow, he knows not how. Of its own accord the land yields fruit, first the blade, then the ear, then the full grain in the ear. And when the grain is ripe, he wields the sickle at once, for the harvest has come. (Mark 4:26-29)

<u>Outer-world:</u>

Jesus is again talking to farm-folk about what is familiar to them: seeds, sprouting, growing, harvesting.

<u>Inner-world:</u>

The story tells that seeds and the kingdom of God grow night and day, so what about nighttime activity: sleep time dreams. Today, dreams are considered helpful for gaining insight into our emotions; what is going on inside us. It is said a picture is worth a thousand words. If this is so, then dreamtime snapshots have much to tell us. One way to relate to dreams is learning to discern the metaphorical ways dreams speak.

Household cats and dogs dream. They make sounds or move legs as if running. Researchers say dreams may sometimes be practicing survival skills. Perhaps the pet is mentally chasing or running away from something. In the complex world of humans, we sometimes chase after, and other times run away from knowing what is going on inside us.

Making choices:

Might harvesting dreams help us ripen more fully into our potential? Is ignoring dreams a missed opportunity for self-knowledge? Do we cheat ourselves and the personality we offer others when we discount the insights dreams can bring? Does lethargy, lack of curiosity, a smug certainty about what we know, keep us from tending to these spontaneous occurrences? Have today's humans outgrown the need for paying attention to dreams, or are we today less evolved psychologically and socially for ignoring our dreams.

Spiritually:

Dreams are important in Judeo-Christianity. In Hebrew scripture, Jacob, Joseph, Solomon, Daniel were profound dreamers. The beginning Christian story includes Joseph's dreams about keeping Mary and infant Jesus safe. Remember the ignored dreams of Pilate's wife.

The earth produces grain through the day and night. So too, humans naturally dream while asleep. The gift of dreams may well help each person participate in and advance the Kingdom of God.

-9-

Sower

A sower went out to sow his seed. And as he sowed, some seed fell on the path and was trampled, and the birds of the sky ate it up. Some fell on rocky ground, and when it grew, it withered for lack of moisture. Some seed fell among thorns, and the thorns grew with it and choked it. And some seed fell on good soil, and when it grew, it produced fruit a hundredfold." After saying this, he called out, "Whoever has ears to hear ought to hear." (Luke 8:4-8)

Outer-world:

This is another parable about seeds and sowing, with three reasons why seeds do not grow, contrasted by what makes seeds produce bountifully.

Inner-world:

Three possible reasons potential new life does not grow in a personality. (1) Being consumed by flighty, superficial, vapid, inane, conventional concerns. (2) Not knowing that psychological thirst can be quenched only by living waters flowing from the depths of one's own soul, (psyche, deep personality). (3) Prickly psychological pain and thorny hurts need healing, otherwise, they choke-out, distrust, and resist the tenderness of grace.

Good psychological soil has to do with open, receptive, teachable attitudes, rich in nourishing possibility and new life. Hearing, listening, understanding with multi-layered subtlety and nuance, is key.

Making choices:

Each of us has a goldfish-in-a-bowl mentality: constricted, restricted, limited. It takes a lifetime of experience to realize how narrow is our perspective. It also takes maturity to realize we cannot know everything, do everything, be everything, in one earthly lifetime. We are therefore bound by commonsense to be humble about what we know and who we are. Humility comes from the Latin word "humus" (soil, earth). Humility is about being down-to-earth, real, genuine, about our capabilities and gift-edness as well as our limitations.

Spiritually:

In the ordinariness of everyday life, wisdom speaks to us, as it did to Jesus in his observations about seeds that wither and seeds that grow – if only we realize that our five senses: hearing, seeing, tasting, touching, smelling, speak psychologically and spiritually, as well as physically. We may thirst for love, see goodness, hunger for kindness, and so on. Metaphor is part of spiritual expression and understanding.

-10-
Parable of Sower Explained

This is the meaning of the parable. The seed is the word of God. Those on the path are the ones who have heard, but the devil comes and takes away the word from their hearts that they may not believe and be saved. Those on rocky ground are the ones who, when they hear, receive the word with joy, but they have no root; they believe only for a time and fall away in time of trial. As for the seed that fell among thorns, they are the ones who have heard, but as they go along, they are choked by the anxieties and riches and pleasures of life, and they fail to produce mature fruit. But as for the seed that fell on rich soil, they are the ones who, when they heard the word,

embrace it with a generous and good heart, and bear fruit through perseverance. (Luke 8:11-15)

<u>Outer-world:</u>

Why does Jesus not give an interpretation for each of his parables as he does here. Perhaps he trusts in the human capacity to "hear" (understand symbolically, figuratively) what his stories and sayings mean throughout the ages.

He says the seed in his parable is the word of God. When Jesus was on earth only Jewish scripture existed, so is the Old Testament the "word of God" to which Jesus is alluding? What else might the "word of God" be? Biblical scholar Raymond E. Brown writes, "Word of God is not simply the word of the Scriptures but certainly includes the Scriptures." [32]

<u>Inner-world:</u>

Explaining this parable, Jesus says the devil takes away the word of God. The devil or Satan is traditionally the embodiment of obstacle, obstruction, blockage of what is valuable and wholesome. At its worst, the devil or Satan is wanton destructive evil. Psychologically, the devil is whatever in the personality interferes with "hearing" (understanding) what is needed to live a fulfilling life. A person can be "off track" with priorities, with lack of perseverance, with immaturities or stunted development, with sabotaging elements in the personality which work against the best in us.

<u>Making choices:</u>

Jesus explains some people were "on the path" before obstacles stopped them. Staying on a spiritual path requires awareness of impediments on the journey, and seeking the grace to replace resistances with correctives. This means facing limitations and weaknesses in the personality which are not fun to recognize, let alone admit to oneself.

Though the truth isn't always pretty, it is necessary, even when painful—sometimes especially when painful—for long-term healing and change. Denial feels better short-term. Sometimes denial is all we can do until we find a more satisfactory way.

---

[32] Raymond E. Brown in *The Virginal Conception & Bodily Resurrection of Jesus,* (New York NY: Paulist Press, 1973), footnote 4, p. 7.

<u>Spiritually:</u>

In Jesus' day, and for some time later, before the terms Christian or Christianity were used, his spiritual movement was referred to as "The Way," indicating a pathway on a journey, which alludes to following interior and exterior habits and ways of being; connected and committed to, cooperating and collaborating with the Spirit of the God-man, Jesus.

-11-
Salt

Salt is good, but if salt itself loses its taste, with what can its flavor be restored? It is fit neither for the soil nor for the manure pile; it is thrown out. Whoever has ears to hear ought to hear. (Luke 14:34)

<u>Outer-world:</u>

Salt has unique qualities that make it both useful and not useful. Salt enhances the flavor of food, but can be detrimental in the soil where it destroys plants or retards their growth. A manure pile with salt in it is unfit as fertilizer because the salt content will contaminate the soil.

<u>Inner-world:</u>

Jesus is dealing with a hypothetical: "If salt itself loses its taste." We can describe mental-emotional states in terms of taste and flavor. Sometimes one can taste the goodness of being alive. Other times, being alive has lost its flavor. It may be that life seems more or less flavorful than it used to be. Salt is the spice which enlivens all other spices; the spice of life, so to speak.

Might Jesus in his salt parable be dealing with a pivotal human problem: not enjoying being alive; a bland existence; mental-emotional depression. This is different from finding meaning and purpose in life despite difficulties and disappointments. Depression is about losing zest for living, feeling useless, without interest, without an appetite for life itself. Jesus could surely sense desperation, despair, depression, in people of his day. Being fully human, he likely experienced such himself.

<u>Making choices:</u>

Is Jesus scolding: "Whoever has ears to hear ought to hear." He may be encouraging, reminding us of our unique human ability to understand life simultaneously on different levels, grasping the similar in the dissimilar, which may not make life delicious

every moment, but certainly more palatable overall. If metaphoric understanding is part
of one's diet of self-discernment, pray that it become more appetizing, even delectable.

Spiritually:

Salt is about more than flavor. It is a food preservative, a disinfectant with
healing properties such as sore throat gargle. Tears are salty; salt is part our biology.
Salt has been used as money-exchange, as ceremonial offering and much more. How-
ever, in this parable Jesus deals with salt as spice, to enhance flavor, to increase the
pleasure of eating. His story is ultimately about finding a radically caring Presence in
the universe with whom one finds life worth savoring rather than a bland, tasteless
existence.

-12-
Tenant Farmers

A man planted a vineyard, leased it to tenant farmers, and then
went on a journey for a long time. At harvest time he sent a servant
to the tenant farmers to receive some of the produce of the vineyard. But they beat the servant and sent him away empty-handed.
So he proceeded to send another servant, but him also they beat
and insulted and sent away empty-handed. Then he proceeded to
send a third, but this one too they wounded and threw out. The
owner of the vineyard said, "What shall I do? I shall send my beloved son; maybe they will respect him." But when the tenant farmers saw him, they said to one another, "This is the heir. Let us kill
him that the inheritance may become ours." So they threw him out
of the vineyard and killed him. What will the owner of the vineyard
do to them? He will come and put those tenant farmers to death
and turn over the vineyard to others." When the people heard this,
they exclaimed, "Let it not be so!" But he looked at them and
asked, "What then does this scripture passage mean?" The stone
which the builders rejected has become the cornerstone. Everyone
who falls on that stone will be dashed to pieces; and it will crush
anyone on whom it falls." (Lk 20:9-18)

Outer-world:

Tenant farmers do not own the land they work. Does this necessarily make them stingy, callous, mean and murderous as this story shows? Notice that eventually the owner also is a death-dealing individual. And what does a cornerstone have to do with a vineyard, for a cornerstone is important in constructing a building, not caring for a vineyard.

Inner-world:

To "own" something; to be an "owner" means to have rights, privileges, and responsibilities related to whatever is owned. This is true in the personality, too, when to "own" or "own-up" is to acknowledge, admit, accept what we know and do not know about the pushes and pulls that go on in our inner world.

Like the tenant farmers in this story, one can be remote from personality ownership, resisting attempts to "own" thoughts, emotions, moods, urges, impulses, unknown parts of who we are. Sometimes defense mechanisms blur, obstruct, hide aspects of the personality. It is natural to be afraid of knowing the unknown roaming about in the personality, even when the unknown is not horrible or reprehensible, but merely unknown.

The owner in this story eventually has a deadly response, so too, fury can possess a personality that is stymied, prevented, closed off from what it needs to know about itself. No one can claim ownership of our personality for us. Only we can "own" (accept) the truths of our personality; what needs to be healed and transformed into gift.

Making choices:

And now for the cornerstone. A cornerstone is the first and critically important reference stone set in a masonry foundation from which all over stones are set, thus determining the shape of the entire structure. Our primary frame of reference (most basic constructs) shapes the personality for better or worse based on experiences not always remembered, but experienced nonetheless; genetically, ancestrally, pre-verbally, unconsciously. The choices we make are built on a foundation which we may or may not understand very well. Because we must make choices, we need awareness about the cornerstone and foundation on which our decisions tend to be made.

Spiritually:

The cornerstone is mentioned in Psalm 118:22 and Isaiah 28:16. In Christianity Jesus is identified as the cornerstone which the builders rejected, and people for different reasons still accept or reject him and what he brought to earth.

His Holy Spirit is always available and if invited into every nook and cranny of the personality, healing the personality becomes really real. That Spirit is our rock, our stone, our foundational reality though the stone also dashes to pieces and crushes incorrect assumptions about oneself, Life, and what we think we know.

-13-
Barren Fig Tree

There once was a person who had a fig tree planted in his orchard, and when he came in search of fruit on it but found none, he said to the gardener, "For three years now I have come in search of fruit on this fig tree but have found none. So cut it down. Why should it exhaust the soil?" He said to him in reply, "Sir, leave it for this year also, and I shall cultivate the ground around it and fertilize it; it may bear fruit in the future. If not you can cut it down." (Luke 13: 6-9)

Outer-world:

Once again, Jesus is using human interaction with plant life and the earth to make a point; to tell a story which has wider, broader, deeper implications than appears at first glance.

Inner-world:

Personality development is a lifetime process which includes big questions. Why are we alive? Why must we die? Why is struggle so constant? Not dealing with such questions or having inadequate answers can leave one restless, unsettled, tossed about by conditions beyond our control, burdened with worry, drowning in a sea of anxiety.

Making choices:

To what degree do we contribute to the fruit our personality brings forth? How much do we need mentors? Can we mentor ourself? Mentoring often comes through books, the words and ideas of others. Over time, one learns to recognize, cooperate and collaborate with grace leading us to what mentors us.

<u>Spiritually:</u>
Jesus, cosmic companion, is a breakthrough evolutionary leap in human consciousness; his kingdom of God is slowly, patiently, evolving on earth, in us, and through us. His Spirit is our personal fertilizer.

-14-
Two Debtors
Two people were in debt to a certain creditor; one owed five hundred days' wages and the other owed fifty. Since they were unable to repay the debt, he forgave it for both. Which of them will love him more?" Simon said in reply, "The one, I suppose, whose larger debt was forgiven." He said to him, "You have judged rightly." (Luke 7:41-43)

<u>Outer-world:</u>
Jesus tells this parable while dining at someone's house where a "sinful woman" bathes his feet with tears, wipes them with her hair, kisses them, anoints them with ointment. The host says to himself that if Jesus is a prophet, he knows the women is a sinner. Then, Jesus tells the parable above.

<u>Inner-world:</u>
Debt, sinfulness, transgression, trespassing are words used in scripture that deal with wrongness, unhealthy, debilitating actions or situations. This is limited vocabulary when dealing with psychological difficulty, and today we have many psychological terms. "Forgiveness" can be about the process of lessening, dissolving, letting go of hurt we carry caused by others, even societal and institutional wrongheadedness, or from other circumstances beyond our control.

<u>Making choices:</u>
Vocabulary has an ethical aspect. How we use vocabulary can be limiting or expansive, creative or destructive. Words, labels, terms liberate and destroy; make us laugh, cry, question, wonder, solve, explain. Jesus' parables in-form psychologically when they "hit home." If the parables are understood only in moralistic tones, they

may not "strike a chord" or "ring a bell" within the personality. Shouldn't we wonder why the woman in this parable is the only one in the room declared "a sinner." Is she the only one "in touch" with her personal desperation? The only one who senses the healing power in Jesus? Above all, is she the only one who has made poor choices? Not likely.

Spiritually:

There is cleverness in this intertwined story about Jesus and his parable. Jesus "knows" the host is thinking that if Jesus is a prophet, he will know the woman is a sinner. Jesus cuts to the crux of the moment when he says to the host, "Simon, I have something to say to you." "Tell me, teacher," Simon says. And Jesus tells the story of the two debtors. Ingeniously, Jesus understands the dynamics in the woman, in Simon, and in the power of being forgiven which lightens our burdens. Great is the human need to have our troubles and afflictions lightened. Perhaps Jesus is always saying to each of us, "I have something to say to you." We do well to answer as Simon did, "Tell me, teacher."

-15-
Rich Fool

There was a rich man whose land produced a bountiful harvest. He asked himself, "What shall I do, for I do not have space to store my harvest?" And he said, "This is what I shall do: I shall tear down my barns and build larger ones. There I shall store all my grain and other goods and I shall say to myself, "Now as for you, you have so many good things stored up for many years, rest, eat, drink, be merry!" But God said to him, "You fool, this night your life will be demanded of you; and the things you have prepared, to whom will they belong?" Thus will it be for the one who stores up treasure for himself but is not rich in what matters to God. (Luke 12:16-21)

Outer-world:

This parable, for the most part, is summed-up in the everyday saying: "You can't take it with you," which is a reality-check concerning our relationship, with "things;" where "things" are on our list of priorities.

Inner-world:

What does matter to God? The primary lesson in Christianity on how to live well, begins with connection to Jesus whose god is caring and utterly concerned with humanity. This primary relationship paves the way for living well with "things." What matters most is that we spend time, energy, effort, on a healthy me-God relationship, involving our whole personality and all its conundrums, so that everything else falls into place better. Then "things" won't be substitutes for unmet needs, unidentified fears and anxieties, unfulfilling attitudes and assumptions that prick and jar us in the depths of our being.

Making-choices:

The Judeo-Christian story is largely about getting humans to act right and live right. Teaching virtue is an old, ongoing, never-ending necessity. Surely, virtue lives alongside psychological dilemmas inside most of us. The caring concern of Jesus' god desires personality healing and wholeness for humanity as well as good character. "Heart" seems to be the biblical term for both character and inmost personality traits. Character and mental-emotional health are related, yet distinct.

Spiritually:

Jesus lived simultaneously in five-sense physical reality and beyond. His parables portray knowledge of what exceeds the material world. In his parables he goes "behind" everyday happenings to the profound. To him five-sense reality is real, but not the only real; five-sense reality is not an end in itself but part of what speech labels infinite, eternal, boundless, the incomprehensible.

-16-
Attitude of a Servant

Who among you would say to your servant who has just come in from plowing or tending sheep in the field, "Come here immediately and take your place at table"? Would he not rather say to him, "Prepare something for me to eat. Put on your apron and wait on me while I eat and drink. You may eat and drink when I am finished"? Is he grateful to that servant because he did what was commanded? So should it be with you. When you have done all you have been commanded, say, "We are unprofitable servants; we have done what we were obliged to do." (Luke 17:7-10)

Outer-world:

This story could be about knowing one's "place" and fulfilling one's obligations in an employment situation, with family, community, or such. It's about a chain of command, and seems to suggest going the extra mile, not merely doing the required minimum.

Inner-world:

The job of servants is to serve. It has recently become popular to talk about wanting to be in service to something greater than ourselves; an ideal, a noble project, a making-life-better enterprise. While this is all well and good, do we know what we are in service to within our personality? What motivates, drives, and compels, or holds us back, gets in our way, sabotages the serenity we crave, leaves unfulfilled our deepest longings. Do we have old memories that need healing, or do old memories that need healing "have" us? Always and everywhere we take our personality with us; we can't leave home without it.

When and how does a personality serve God? The old phrase "to do the will of God" assumes we know God's intentions and have the ability to carry them out. Another way to phrase this idea is to talk about the unique contribution each human brings to earth in her or his being. Yet we know that life on earth is flawed, and sometimes our own psychological factors disrupt, impede, block, wreck, the best intentions to be of service.

Making choices:

A capable servant performs with a sense of duty, obligation, responsibility, accountability, dependability, discipline. Honorable stuff, we might say at first glance. And honorable are these traits when serving what is good, noble, healthy, creative. However, when serving psychologically damaged or sick motives, these potentially fine character traits can be especially, and even efficiently, destructive. Morality and personality are intertwined, yet separate.

Spiritually:

Religious talk about piety and morality can obscure the role played by personality in cooperating with Christ to build a new creation: a world of justice and love, peace and nonviolence, which begins with the human personality; its hurts, hindrances, and hopes.

-17-

Persistent Widow

There was a judge in a certain town who neither feared God nor respected any human being. And a widow in that town used to come to him and say, "Render a just decision for me against my adversary." For a long time the judge was unwilling, but eventually he thought, "While it is true that I neither fear God nor respect any human being, because this widow keeps bothering me I shall deliver a just decision for her lest she finally come and strike me." (Luke 18:1-5)

Friend at Midnight

Suppose one of you has a friend to whom he goes at midnight and says, "Friend, lend me three loaves of bread, for a friend of mine has arrived at my house from a journey and I have nothing to offer him," and he says in reply from within, "Do not bother me; the door has already been locked and my children and I are already in bed. I cannot get up to give you anything." I tell you, if he does not get up to give him the loaves because of their friendship, he will get up to give him whatever he needs because of his persistence. (Luke 11:5-8)

Outer-world:

These two stories are about persistency and expediency. So, keep pestering someone until we get what we want, for the person being pestered may well give in, not because it's the right thing to do, but because it's the expedient thing to do; he wants to get rid of someone hounding him.

The lesson gleaned from these stories is to be persistent in prayer. However, is God like humans and expediently gives in to human requests if we but hassle and hound enough?

Inner-world:

The idea of hounding God brings to mind a famous hounding poem with a radically different development. The poem is "Hound of Heaven" by Francis Thompson (1859-1907), an English poet addicted to opium; homeless at times. The poem shows divine love doggedly hunting down the poet, relentlessly pursuing him and his burdens — while the poet flees from his rescuer. Thompson's 182-line poem begins:

I fled him down the nights and down the days
I fled him down the arches of the years
I fled him down the labyrinthine ways
Of my own mind, and in the midst of tears . . .

Not all tears are shed outwardly, but inwardly. We often flee from knowing our inmost tears; the twists and turns of mind and emotions which include bruises, confused priorities, attachments askew, loves unrequited, aching for the source of love itself.

Making choices:

Ignoring personality pain has consequences. Ignoring doesn't make the pain go away but makes the personality ignorant about itself. Expedient ways to rid oneself of nagging personality pain are to appease by giving-in to easy explanations; indulging in short-term solutions; distracting oneself, white-washing, denying personality issues. Expedient, short-term solutions have long-term compounding consequences.

The rageful personality remains trapped in rage; the hopeless personality in desperation; the addictive personality in addiction, the frightened personality is stuck in fear. Meanwhile, others are pelted by fallout from these pockets of personality in need of tending. Sometimes the primary person cannot or will not deal with their maladies, and so, others must pay. We all must pray about each other's maladies; and especially our own.

Spiritually:

All of life cannot be reduced to psychology, yet everyday personality (soul) is too often left-out of Christian consideration. The idea of an immortal soul sometimes receives more attention than everyday soul (deep personality).

Jesus is said to have healed hemorrhaging, blindness, the lame, and lepers. Are we not all psychologically blind in some areas of our life, or lame, unable to move about creatively, suffering from psychological sores and wounds, or emotionally bleeding? The healing hound of heaven waits for us to stop running and avoiding; to end the chase, and experience the embrace of grace in psychological, deep personality, soul-healing.

-18-

Tree Known by its Fruit

A good tree does not bear rotten fruit, nor does a rotten tree bear good fruit. For every tree is known by its own fruit. For people do not pick figs from thorn bushes, nor do they gather grapes from brambles. A good person out of the store of goodness in his heart produces good, but an evil person out of a store of evil produces evil; for from the fullness of the heart the mouth speaks. (Luke 6:43-45)

Outer-world:

Strict literalism might conclude comparing a human with a tree is a waste of time and energy. Yet, Jesus's analogy bears its own fruit.

Inner-world:

Fig trees and humans do both bear fruit; each "speaks," "shows itself" by what it produces. And there are more likenesses. Each has roots below the surface, not directly observable. Also, humans have outer personalities just as trees have bark on their trunks to protect the inmost part of the tree's trunk which is labeled "heartwood."

Biblically, the inmost part of the personality is often referred to as "heart." We still say "with all my heart," indicating something especially essential and vital. We use many heart words and heart phrases: heartily, heartfelt, heartache, heartbroken, heartless, light-hearted, cross one's heart, cry one's heart out, get to the heart of, have one's heart in one's throat, have one's heart in the right place, to lose heart, to take heart, to wear one's heart on one's sleeve, with all one's heart, to speak heart to heart.

Today, the word "unconscious" is used instead of the word "heart" which in ancient thought was considered the seat of the emotions. The parable above is compatible with the idea that emotions we are not aware of (unconscious) greatly influence not only what our mouth speaks, but everything else about us. Emotions, pleasant and unpleasant, comfortable and uncomfortable, are much of who and what we are.

Emotions are embodied, physiological reactions (however miniscule), from memories including pre-verbal memories, present happenings, and future possibilities including priorities and expectations. We are always and everywhere evaluating existence: past, present, future.

Making choices:

No matter how mature, a tree cannot make choices about soil, water or sunlight in which it grows and develops. However, adult humans must make choices: healthy, unhealthy and everything in-between.

Our family tree (genetics) determines part of our temperament, and so does what we are taught, how we are trained by those who model their behavior to us, events that shape us, condition and predispose us towards what we do, especially with our emotions.

Today we may not memorize lists of virtues: prudence, justice, temperance, fortitude, humility, generosity, love, kindness, chastity, charity, faith, zeal, hopefulness, affection, truth, ingenuity, modesty, honesty, fairness, steadfastness, courage, patience, loyalty, felicity (to name a few). Today there is more talk about short-term and long-term consequences of choices. Perhaps virtues have become embedded in the process of making mature decisions.

Spiritually:

Jesus' beloved Kingdom, which he foresaw and was optimistic about making a pervasive earthly reality, is based on the healthy human personality. Perhaps this is at the center of his fig tree analogy. Jesus' teachings are aimed at changing the world, beginning with the fruit each brings forth from healthy depths of one's being, connected to Creativity Itself, which Jesus in his patriarchal culture referred to as Father.

-19-
Two Foundations

Why do you call me, "Lord, Lord," but not do what I command? I will show you what someone is like who comes to me, listens to my words, and acts on them. That one is like a person building a house, who dug deeply and laid the foundation on rock; when the flood came, the river burst against that house but could not shake it because it had been well built. But the one who listens and does not act is like a person who built a house on the ground without a foundation. When the river burst against it, it collapsed at once and was completely destroyed. (Luke 6:46-49)

Outer-world:

A practical person knows a stable house (or any building) must be built on a stable foundation. Rock is firm and solid; sand easily shifts and gives way. What kind of person listens and acts on the words of Jesus?

Inner-world:

Jesus, person of evolved consciousness, speaks to his "followers" about being superficial; not foundationally involved with what he offers. Rather than scolding, he is sharing what he knows well from his own experience, which is that perfunctory, token, dutiful acquiescence in spirituality and religion is not what humans need.

His story invites the question of where one goes within the personality in times of distress or crisis? Is there a rock bottom, unshakeable, steadfast premise, thought, conviction, ultimate source that helps one through the many storms life brings? Where does one find solace in turmoil, peace despite conflict, a place we go psychologically in situations so difficult we spontaneously gasp, "Oh, my god."

Jesus is saying he is the One on whom we can depend for sanity, for survival; the foundation on which our constructs and overall frame of reference can be safely built; a bulwark and buffer against the external storms of the world, and the internal storms of the personality.

Making choices:

The one who listens but does not act suggests distant relationship, detached involvement; a spectator; knowing about Jesus, but not experiencing him as rock bottom reality in one's bones, in deep personality which needs profound understanding in contrast to being covered-over by platitudinous chatter. Such honesty requires moral courage.

Spiritually:

Jesus has titles: Lord, Savior, Redeemer. Judaism has different names for God: Yahweh, Elohim, El, Shaddai, Adoni (Adoni is translated "Lord"). The Jewish God was a personalized god, not an abstract notion. Jesus is an historical person; a breakthrough individual who penetrated and opened the door of ultimate reality for the rest of us to walk through; a foundation on which to build our personality, our life.

-20-

Yeast

To what shall I compare the kingdom of God? It is like yeast that a woman took and mixed [in] with three measures of wheat flour until the whole batch of dough was leavened. (Luke 13:20-21)

Outer-world:

Yeast in dough permeates, infuses, pervades, saturates, soaks, infiltrates, invades, spreads throughout, for better or worse, and cannot be extracted, taken-out. Yeast permanently, unalterably, changes the dough and causes it to rise, to increase in size. In Hebrew and most of Christian scripture, yeast has a bad reputation representing negative influence. However, practically speaking, yeast simply changes the character of dough.

Inner-world:

It is helpful to wonder what unknowingly permeates one's personality like yeast. What shadow elements, both positive and negative, suffuse one's being; are spread within having their influence outside. These may be unresolved issues or underdeveloped potential of parents or other generational influences; perhaps lost childhood curiosity or enthusiasm for being alive; unrealized capacity for receiving and giving love; untapped desire for God.

We are more than we know. The yeast within can puff us up, but as punctured dough, leave us deflated, flattened by life's woundings. Also, bread is basic sustenance and yeast can represent expansion, rising to new heights, having more to share with others. And so we grow, experiencing everyday highs and lows.

Making choices:

The Kingdom of God is like yeast, the parable says. Apparently, this kingdom of compassionate wisdom spreads through humanity, one person at a time, with healthy ways of being and living, bringing a paradigm of increased consciousness to the planet. Though already underway, who knows how long it will take for Jesus' life of creative compassionate consciousness to become the dominate way of life on earth; for the yeast of loving wisdom to spread and become the status quo. Though flour does not resist yeast, humans can resist increasing consciousness about oneself.

Jesus, the Bread of Life, permeates humanity personality-by-personality. His Spirit is like yeast spreading within, amongst, and throughout those who receive him consciously, conscientiously.

-21-
Vigilant and Faithful

Be sure of this: if the master of the house had known the hour when the thief was coming, he would not have let his house be broken into. You also must be prepared, for at an hour you do not expect, the Son of Man will come. (Luke 12:39-40)

Outer-world:

Is Jesus comparing himself to a thief? Are we to steel ourselves against Him, who steals into people's lives when they are unaware?

Inner-world:

This story is opposite of what first seems to be the case. The lesson is likely about becoming vigilant of subtle, nuanced, unpleasant thoughts and feelings stealing into prominence in our personality (our home—where we really live) robbing us of contentment and enjoyment. "Be prepared" may allude not only to these disquieting moments and moods, but to our capacity to perceive with subtly and nuance the countless spontaneous opportunities when grace restores psychic equilibrium.

Making choices:

Personal vigilance is a choice. It's about being smart and discerning about what is in our thoughts and emotions which can destroy a hopeful zest about being alive. Crisp discernment is a far cry from morbid introspection or narcissistic preoccupation. It takes courage to willingly encounter our psyche, to choose learning about our personality.

Spiritually:

Who or what is the Son of Man in the story? Over centuries, much has been written about the title, Son of Man. Jesus might simply be saying he himself is fully human. This fully-human, fully-divine individual is the core of Christianity, and so is the recognition of humanity's potential for accessing and absorbing divinity, however remote that possibility seems when looking at much of human history, daily news troubles, and one's own limitations. Yet, humanity's awareness and compassion is and evolves.

-22-
Dinner Invitations

A man gave a great dinner to which he invited many. When the time for the dinner came, he dispatched his servant to say to those invited, "Come, everything is now ready." But one by one, they all began to excuse themselves. The first said to him, "I have purchased a field and must go to examine it; I ask you, consider me excused." And another said, "I have purchased five yoke of oxen and am on my way to evaluate them; I ask you, consider me excused." And another said, "I have just married a woman, and therefore I cannot come." The servant went and reported this to his master. Then the master of the house in a rage commanded his servant, "Go out quickly into the streets and alleys of the town and bring in here the poor and the crippled, the blind and the lame." The servant reported, "Sir, your orders have been carried out and still there is room.' The master then ordered the servant, "Go out to the highways and hedgerows and make people come in that my home may be filled. For, I tell you, none of these men who were invited will taste my dinner." (Luke 14:16-24)

Outer-world:

The invited guests declined because they were busy with practical matters. The man giving the dinner seems overly sensitive and excessively offended. His priority becomes filling his home with anyone available, and having a punitive attitude toward those who decline his invitation.

Inner-world:

This can be a story of conflicting dynamics within a personality, for each of us is filled with a banquet of pushes and pulls; a complex feast of opposite tendencies and approaches for tasting the richness which life offers. Out of this abundance, each personality develops some traits more than others.

Some personalities are more introverted, others more extraverted. Each develops unique patterns of gathering, processing, and organizing information about life and living. One individual is more thinking than feeling, or vice versa. Another, more intuitive than sensate, or the other way round. Some seek closure, others open-endedness.

Some are more nourished by "things." Others are energized by "ideas," "people," "creativity," "spirituality," and so on. Even cultures have preferences, and preferences may serve well but not completely. In preference there is lopsidedness. Underdeveloped traits and qualities become the "poor and the crippled, the blind and the lame" (neglected or devalued aspects of personality and culture). Every psychological part must be brought to the table (the table of the Lord) for healing and wholeness.

Making choices:

This is a story about paradox in the personality. While one is busy functioning, using well-developed personality traits and qualities, in the end underdeveloped aspects of the personality, those areas where we are psychologically needy, weak, deficient, uncomfortable, tend to bring us to feast with the divine. Recognizing our psychological poverty opens the door to abundance. This is a strange truth which takes moral courage to fully admit.

Spiritually:

The host in the story is determined to fill his home with guests. He wants only to share his dinner with them; to have them "taste" his food. Messiah Jesus brought his Messianic banquet to humankind, and we are all invited to dine with him, no matter our types of impoverishment, the ways in which we are crippled, blind or lame, or where we come from (the highways and hedgerows) genetically, geographically, temperamentally, educationally. All parts of us are invited to dine with him.

-23-
Return of an Unclean Spirit

When an unclean spirit goes out of someone, it roams through arid regions searching for rest but, finding none, it says, "I shall return to my home from which I came." But upon returning, it finds it swept clean and put in order. Then it goes and brings back seven other spirits more wicked than itself who move in and dwell there,

and the last condition of that person is worse than the first." (Luke 11:24-26)

Outer-world:

In the world of Jesus' days on earth, what we today consider problematic psychological dynamics were labeled "unclean spirits."

Inner-world:

Today, we have many diagnostic categories and labels regarding psychological disorders. We speak of chemical imbalances, repressions, complexes, traumas, negative memories, thoughts, emotions. The primary lesson in the parable may be this: trying to remove undesirable elements in a personality without fostering creative elements at the same time, creates an existential vacuum (a clean room), for more "'spirits' to move in and dwell."

The removal of an addiction or psychological disorder is not enough by itself; the pursuit of meaning, purpose, finding one's unique and valued existence is needed. Simplistic approaches to the wondrous complexity of the human personality are not helpful. Jesus understood the human need for meaning, having a meaningful existence.

Making choices:

Guilt and shame are natural and healthy psychological reactions to our destructive behaviors, and poor choices. There can also be neurotic guilt and shame, which is neither natural or healthy, but confused and unhealthy. Healing and forgiveness involve discerning legitimate from invalid guilt and shame. We must be rock-bottom honest and real about guilt and shame, for we are capable of both clear perception and conniving deception.

Spiritually:

It's impossible to believe the world can be renewed without the depths of the human personality (the biblical "heart") being renewed, healed, transformed one-by-one into Godlikeness. "Theoria," "theosis," are Greek words dealing with Christian "divinization" of the human personality.

Judge for Yourselves
Why do you not judge for yourselves what is right? If you are to go with your opponent before a magistrate, make an effort to settle the matter on the way; otherwise your opponent will turn you over to the judge, and the judge hand you over to the constable, and the constable throw you into prison. I say to you, you will not be released until you have paid the last penny. (Luke 12:58-59)

<u>Outer-world:</u>
It is least expensive and therefore wisest to settle disputes out-of-court.

<u>Inner-world:</u>
Imagine the opponent in this story is an aspect within one's own personality, for we have opposing dynamics within the personality, which at their best are, all together, part of our survival kit. Each trait can potentially serve us well, but can also become compromised, twisted, convoluted, inflated, diminished, malfunctioning, and work against our best interests. Paradoxically, even our greatest personality strength is sometimes our greatest personality weakness. Example: an ability to be organized can become a strident, bossy, critical attitude towards anyone not well-organized, though a deficient organizer may greatly exceed the critical one in other areas of development.

This parable suggests it is best to consciously deal with personal psychological adversaries sooner rather than later. The more we put off dealing with personality traits that sabotage us, the greater the likelihood our psychological saboteurs will deal with us, undermining, standing in the way, jeopardizing the quality of life available to us, for which we pay dearly.

<u>Making choices:</u>
The parable begins by asking, "Why do you not judge for yourselves what is right?" Apparently, we sometimes have more discernment than we want; we hide from truth available to us. We'd rather "not know."

Wanting to see all aspects of our personality takes effort; disturbs our comfort zone (ego); punctures our prideful status-quo arrogance about who we have decided we are. I'm not talking now about uncovering personality traits that are criminal and obvious. With the not so obvious, it takes courage to seek more and more truth about the totality of who we are and can become; to search for self-knowledge.

<u>Spiritually:</u>

Can we depend on God to be gentle with us if we search for self-knowledge? We don't want to be overwhelmed with too much unpleasant, painful, psychological material. Can we be sure God is the gentle strength Jesus displayed? Jesus has a side of tenderness appealing to humans, yet the story of his crucifixion and death is brutal, and we may want to shrink from too much God-connection if such can result.

The historical human story includes many atrocities. Despite this, and maybe in reaction to the atrocities, the overall growth of personal consciousness continues to evolve. Meanwhile, each of us can individually, quietly, unceremoniously, add to the quality of life on earth, (without waiting for the social system, the legal system, or whatever collective system, to catch-up), by inviting the tenderness of Jesus to walk with us through personality tensions, internal conflicts, distorted priorities, unresolved issues.

-25-
Good Samaritan

A scholar of the law said to Jesus, "And who is my neighbor?" Jesus replied, "A man fell victim to robbers as he went down from Jerusalem to Jericho. They stripped and beat him and went off leaving him half-dead. A priest happened to be going down that road, but when he saw him, he passed by on the opposite side. Likewise, a Levite came to the place, and when he saw him, he passed by on the opposite side. But a Samaritan traveler who came upon him was moved with compassion at the sight. He approached the victim, poured oil and wine over his wounds and bandaged them. Then he lifted him up on his own animal, took him to an inn and cared for him. The next day he took out two silver coins and gave them to the innkeeper with the instruction, "Take care of him. If you spend more than what I have given you, I shall repay you on my way back." Which of these three in your opinion, was neighbor to the robbers' victim?" He answered, "The one who treated him with mercy." Jesus said to him, "Go and do likewise." (Luke 10:19-37)

Outer-world:
Being a neighbor is not just about physical geography or living nearby.

Inner-world:

Will we ever be more intimately near to anyone than our own inner being? Have we not all been beaten-up by life to some extent? Do I not sometimes beat-up on myself? Can we assume that so long as we don't do awful things, commit big sins, we don't have psychological wounds that need bandaging and care? Wounds such as feelings of inferiority, insecurity, anger, rage, chronic irritation, exaggerated fears, blockages related to receiving and giving love, callous indifference towards others, laziness, irresponsibility, ongoing deceptions and dishonesties, festering bitterness or jealousies, self-loathing, inflated arrogance, unrelenting frustrations, lingering embarrassment or humiliation in trivial matters, uneasiness with others, uneasiness being alone, lack of motivation or interest, extreme self-absorption, poor choices and decisions, exaggerated psychological or physical aggression, disproportionate neediness, too compliant or stubborn, inability to contribute to the welfare of self and others, addictive tendencies, bothersome impulses and cravings, undue influence of unhealthy social fads, screwed-up priorities, etc. We all experience dis-ease in various ways.

While diversity in personality makes the world go around, there are personality abilities, disabilities, and liabilities.

Making choices:

Being left half-dead, and being saved through compassion, are at the center of this story in which two religious personages, a priest and a Levite, go to the opposite side of the road to avoid dealing with the injured man. Is this story telling us to not hide behind religion, not use religion to avoid noticing certain dynamics in our personality in need of healing which rob us of the fullness of life?

Spiritually:

The "neighbor" in this story is the one who is merciful to a stranger. Are we not sometimes strangers to ourself? We can extrapolate that it is merciful to tend to the injured, wounded, psychologically bleeding parts of our own personality, even if the Christianity we have been taught has often ignored, by-passed, not sufficiently appreciated the universal human need for psychological healing, including our own.

-26-

Choice of Place at Table

When you are invited by someone to a wedding banquet, do not recline at table in the place of honor. A more distinguished guest than you may have been invited by him, and the host who invited

both of you may approach you and say, "Give your place to this man,' and then you would proceed with embarrassment to take the lowest place. Rather, when you "My friend, move up to a higher position." Then you will enjoy the esteem of your companions at the table. For everyone who exalts himself will be humbled, but the one who humbles himself will be exalted. (Luke 14:7-11)

Outer-world:

This is a story about social customs, proper manners, doing the correct thing so as to not embarrass. Social position, class status, peer approval, trappings of authority and honor, whether merit-based or dictated by tradition or power are facts of life which must be dealt with.

Inner-world:

In this parable, Jesus is talking about more than seating etiquette at a wedding banquet. The final sentence holds an important lesson. "For everyone who exalts himself will be humbled, but the one who humbles himself will be exalted." In psychology, the phrase "ego inflation" is used when someone elevates, exaggerates what they think they know, or the power they have. We all engage in ego inflation at times, and know how humiliating it feels later, when we are not so inflated ("full of ourself"), when we are more genuine, down-to-earth, real about ourself. Ego inflation may arise out of insecurity, or from the arrogance of insufficient experience. Ego inflation is a kind of immaturity unable to evaluate itself adequately. Becoming aware of our ego inflations is one of life's great lessons but not a fun time, for we feel bruised by the truth, the embarrassment of recognizing this kind of puffed-up fakeness in our own personality; our own behavior.

Making choices:

This parable is about exalting oneself, seeking esteem, and being humiliated, all at the same time. Much of life involves these complex components involving risk: to risk being who we are, who we want to be, how we wish to be seen by others. Psychological risk requires uncommon wisdom on a situation-by-situation basis, is a big part of choices we must make, and has us endlessly needing God's grace.

Spiritually:

In this parable, a conventional marriage has taken place. However, I now risk suggesting a different kind of marriage in the personality: learning to recognize both hemispheres of one's brain.

To Christians, Jesus is someone who intimately and profoundly knew himself and his mission in life. He could debate the learned people of his day because of his intuitive right-hemisphere knowing, mixed with analytic left-hemisphere ability. He was not educated in the way we think of education, yet possessed wisdom far superior to mere information-gathering. He could intuit and synthesize (right-hemisphere abilities) practical elements of daily life, and then organize and articulate (left-hemisphere abilities) the connections he saw between five-sense reality and spiritual reality into profound life lessons in his parables.

We can more easily risk fulfilling our psychological potential for discerning how, what, when, where, whether to risk, if we are familiar with what is now known about traits and qualities of both hemispheres of the brain. Then we may not so easily stumble over our own psychological lopsidedness.

-27-
Vigilant Servants

Gird your loins and light your lamps and be like servants who await their master's return from a wedding, ready to open immediately when he comes and knocks. Blessed are those servants whom the master finds vigilant on his arrival. Amen, I say to you, he will gird himself, have them recline at table, and proceed to wait on them. And should he come in the second or third watch and find them prepared in this way, blessed are those servants. (Luke12:35-38)

Outer-world:

This is again, a commonsense lesson on being willing servants, rewarded by their master for their vigilance by his serving them. Originally, girding one's loins was about tying or arranging the robe or garment one was wearing so it wouldn't get in the way while working. Today the phrase "girding one's loins" still means getting ready to work or to tackle something strenuous. Lighting a lamp is turning on light so we can "see."

Inner-world:

The setting of the story is nighttime, after a wedding. Speaking psychologically, a wedding or marriage can symbolize aspects of the personality coming together. Likewise, turning on the light can allude to becoming conscious of something we've been "in the dark" about; girding one's loins may suggest the willingness, effort and endurance to seek personality transformation; the master serving the servants could indicate significant changes in personality dynamics.

For example, some personalities prefer "closure," which is coming to a decision, making a choice, having a situation or understanding wrapped-up, finished, over and done with. Other personalities are more drawn to various options, more possibilities, points-of-view, open-endedness. Either closure or open-endedness can serve well, but sometimes an individual can be stuck in one or the other approach, in which case, a conscious change to use both approaches will serve better, depending on the situation. Part of wisdom is knowing when to seek closure and when the open-ended approach is best, thus integrating (marrying) the two approaches.

<u>Making choices:</u>
Perhaps the greatest choices we make in life are about offering our total personality for transformation in God's light and love.

<u>Spiritually:</u>
The parable emphasizes "blessed servants." The "second or third watch" is nighttime when one is typically sleeping and dreaming. We dream about every ninety minutes while asleep, whether or not we pay attention to our dreams.

Today, dreams are generally thought to be about the individual dreamer, whereas in tribal cultures significant dreams about the welfare of the group came to particularly "gifted" people (such as a medicine man or woman — a shaman) in the group. It is safe to trust dreams as a safe avenue for personal wisdom so long as they are regarded symbolically, metaphorically, not literally.

-28-
Dishonest Steward

A rich man had a steward who was reported to him for squandering his property. He summoned him and said, "What is this I hear about you? Prepare a full account of your stewardship, because you can no longer be my steward." The steward said to himself, "What shall I do, now that my master is taking the position of steward

away from me? I am not strong enough to dig and I am ashamed
to beg. I know what I shall do so that, when I am removed from
the stewardship, they may welcome me into their homes." He
called in his master's debtors one by one. To the first he said, "How
much do you owe my master?" He replied, "One hundred
measures of olive oil." He said to him, "Here is your promissory
note. Sit down and quickly write one for fifty." Then to another he
said, "And you, how much do you owe?" He replied, "One hundred kors of wheat." He said to him, 'Here is your promissory note;
write one for eighty." And the master commended that dishonest
steward for acting prudently. (Luke 16: 1-8)

Outer-world:
*It seems strange that the master praises his dishonest steward for acting prudently.
However, at the time of Jesus on earth, agents working on behalf of their masters,
charged their own fees on transactions. So when this fellow got fired for some other
dishonesty, he had debtors rewrite their notes minus his fees. Therefore, the master was
still getting what was owed him. This is why the master commended the dishonest
steward. Plus, subtracting his fees made the debtors feel favorably toward him. He
shrewdly planned on their future friendliness towards him.*

*Jesus explains this parable in various ways. One comment he makes is, "The
person who is trustworthy in very small matters is also trustworthy in great ones; and
the person who is dishonest in very small matters is also dishonest in great ones."*
(Luke 16: 10)

Inner-world:
*Psychologically, it is possible to be honest or dishonest with oneself, in small and
large ways. Honesty with oneself is related to how much we are connected to the mystery
within our own being; the inmost aspects of the personality. Yet it seems our everyday
mindset (ego) is limited in how much it knows about the innermost events of the personality (emotions, moods, cravings, yearnings). Sleeptime dreams can figuratively show
us interior events in the personality.*

*During REM (rapid eye movement) sleep, there is high activation in the brain's
amygdala, which is the seat of intense emotional reactions. In dreaming we seem to be
trying to integrate and come to terms with emotional difficulties. Dreaming may be an
internal therapist, helping us integrate emotional experiences at the present time. The*

brain's limbic system, the command center for directing emotion and storing strong emotional memory, directs the dream show.

Making choices:

Is paying attention to one's sleeptime dreams a moral duty? Are most people willing to pay regular attention to their dreams? Probably not. Despite this, the effort of dealing with dreams provides opportunities for self-knowledge which can lead to greater personality harmony. If relating to dreams with symbolic savvy becomes wide-spread, there just might be more peace on earth in individuals, families, the whole human family.

Spiritually:

The ex-employee in this parable "out-smarted" himself, so to speak. His dishon-esty seems to have worked against him; complicated his life. He demonstrates a complex personality. We all have complex personalities full of opposing tendencies, which are part of our survival kit. This Jesus story reveals Jesus is a realist about the complexity of personality traits and the complexity of human survival. Jesus says honesty or dis-honesty is a habit, an attitude, a personality disposition. Pray to become conscious of helpful dispositions, and for the awareness and transformation of unhelpful attitudes.

-29-
Pharisee and Tax Collector

Two people went up to the temple area to pray; one was a Pharisee and the other was a tax collector. The Pharisee took up his position and spoke this prayer to himself, "O God, I thank you that I am not like the rest of humanity—greedy, dishonest, adulterous—or even like this tax collector. I fast twice a week, and I pay tithes on my whole income." But the tax collector stood off at a distance and would not even raise his eyes to heaven but beat his breast and prayed, O God, be merciful to me a sinner." I tell you, the latter went home justified, not the former; for everyone who exalts him-self will be humbled, and the one who humbles himself will be ex-alted. (Luke 18:9-14)

Outer-world:

In this parable Jesus is concerned with thoughts; not external behaviors, but thoughts.

Inner-world:

There may be various Pharisees and tax collectors in each of us: Pharisee parts of us feel "better than," and tax collector parts in us feel "not as good as." We juggle, weigh, gauge, assess, our real-self against our ideal-self; against others. Our limited ego goes back and forth trying to size-up our worth, our value, how we measure our inadequacies, fears, troubles, confusions, regrets, sorrows, insecurities, against a plethora of pleasant, enjoyable, desired personality possibilities.

Generally, the tax collector part of us is in touch with undesirable aspects of our personality and can easily admit we are not perfect, whereas the Pharisee part of us sees our strengths compared with others' shortcomings while remaining "in the dark" about shadow elements that may have their way with us without our realizing this.

Making choices:

How responsible are we for what we think when many uninvited thoughts spontaneously "pop into our head." A beginning responsibility is becoming aware of unasked-for thoughts; brain chatter that seems to have a life of its own.

Spiritually:

In this parable, the tax collector's attitude is favored. In the bible, this attitude is sometimes labeled, "a contrite heart." Otherwise, dominating thought patterns of feeling "better than" keeps one blind to grace already received; and grace still needed.

-30-
Life after Death

There was a rich man who dressed in purple garments and fine linen and dined sumptuously each day. And lying at his door was a poor man named Lazarus, covered with sores, who would gladly have eaten his fill of the scraps that fell from the rich man's table. Dogs even used to come and lick his sores. When the poor man died, he was carried away by angels to the bosom of Abraham. The rich man also died and was buried, and from the netherworld, where he was in torment, he raised his eyes and saw Abraham far off and Lazarus at his side. And he cried out, "Father Abraham, have pity on me. Send Lazarus to dip the tip of his finger in water and cool my tongue, for I am suffering torment in these flames." Abraham replied, "My child, remember that you received what was good during your lifetime while Lazarus likewise received what was bad; but now he is comforted here, whereas you are tormented. Moreover, between us and you a great chasm is established to prevent anyone from crossing who might wish to go from our side to yours or from your side to ours." He said, "Then I beg you, father, send him to my father's house, for I have five brothers, so that he may warn them, lest they too come to this place of torment." But Abraham replied, "They have Moses and the prophets. Let them listen to them." He said, "Oh no, father Abraham, but if someone from the dead goes to them, they will repent." Then Abraham said, "If they will not listen to Moses and the prophets, neither will they be persuaded if someone should rise from the dead." (Luke 16:19-31)

Outer-world:

We don't know whether the rich man earned his wealth in an honest way, obtained it fraudulently, or inherited it. We don't know whether the poor man couldn't or wouldn't provide better for himself. We only know after death the poor man is comforted and the rich man is tormented. Is wealth always dishonorable and poverty honorable? What specifically had the rich man done that was so wrong? Why does a great chasm in the afterlife exist to keep the comforted and tormented apart? Though these are questions to ask about the story, what is not questioned is whether there is life after death. In this story, ongoing life is assumed.

The story ends with a comment about people not listening to Moses and the prophets, or even someone rising from the dead, an obvious reference to Jesus's resurrection. Once again, life is assumed to continue after death.

Inner-world:

In the story the rich man and poor man seemingly continue to be individuals after death; they retain their identities. We know at death the body dies, but what about the personality (the soul; the immortal soul)? Is the idea of purgatory a way to suggest the human personality continues to evolve after death? Would I want my present personality to continue throughout eternity? What might I want changed? What aspects am I comfortable with now? The parable shows physical comforts are no guarantee against psycho-spiritual torments.

Making choices:

What is causing the rich man's torment in the parable? Was indifference to someone else's suffering his deficiency? Was he jaded, unaware, blind, insensitive, clueless, lacking concern about another's situation? How could the rich man with a life of material privilege, and we assume for the story does not say otherwise, with the human ability to think, reason, feel, understand, not be more responsive, empathetic, generous, towards the poor man.

The rich man wants cool water for his tongue in his inflamed psycho-spiritual state. As for the tongue: did the rich man ever "say" anything while on earth to help suffering humanity? Did the rich man every "say" prayers for struggling humanity? What we "say" in thoughts, words, and deeds, makes a difference in self and others.

The rich man wants someone to "warn" his five brothers; he is still wanting advantage for his inner circle, his cohorts, those close to him, his own kind, his tribe, what he values.

Spiritually:

The parable does not say this, but perhaps life after death involves total consciousness, complete awareness of one's earthly life, one's personality; what was possible and what was not realized, and therein lies one's torment or comfort.

Jesus' stories prod and poke at humanity, stretching each of us towards the person we can fully become: creative, helpful, hopeful, making life better for all creatures and creation, close to us and far away.

-31-
Wheat and Weeds

The kingdom of heaven may be likened to a man who sowed good seed in his field. While everyone was asleep his enemy came and sowed weeds all through the wheat, and then went off. When the crop grew and bore fruit, the weeds appeared as well. The slaves of the householder came to him and said, "Master, did you not sow good seed in your field? Where have the weeds come from?" He answered, "An enemy has done this." His slaves said to him, "Do you want us to go and pull them up?" He replied, "No, if you pull up the weeds you might uproot the wheat along with them. Let them grow together until harvest; then at harvest time I will say to the harvesters, "First collect the weeds and tie them in bundles for burning; but gather the wheat into my barn." (Matthew 13:24-30)

Outer-world:

A practical lesson in this parable is to not destroy a valuable crop while attempting to get rid of weeds.

Inner-world:

Every personality is a mix of wheat and weeds, speaking figuratively. It takes a lifetime of good and smart cultivation for some personality "weeds" to be transformed into a crop of positive traits and tendencies; for weeds (undesirable characteristics) to change or dissipate over time.

Mentioned earlier, there is the paradox that in certain circumstances our greatest strength is also our greatest weakness, and our greatest weakness can potentially become our greatest strength. Depending on the circumstance, stubbornness may be helpful, or a hindrance. An efficient person is not always an effective person, and the other way round. Can we always be sure who our enemy is in the personality? Transforming the personality is more real and healthy than a goal of eradicating aspects of the personality, which, even if possible, diminishes the personality. Transformation is the goal, not eradication.

Making choices:

This parable deals with patience, maturity, waiting for the right time when making choices, solving problems. It's a way of saying the first or most obvious solution is not always the best solution, as Jesus makes clear when he says you might uproot the wheat when you pull up the weeds. However, by the time the wheat is ripe for harvest its roots are deeper and it is less easily pulled-up, plus the wheat's mature appearance makes it easier to distinguish from the mature weeds (darnel), and thus the wheat is less likely to be accidentally destroyed.

Just as mature wheat and mature darnel look less alike than when they were young plants, so too waiting, watching with patient endurance, often sharpens contrasts in a situation, making a decision more informed.

Spiritually:

Jesus tells us in this tale of wheat and weeds, that a man sowed good seed, but while everyone was asleep, his enemy came and sowed weeds. Notice: "while everyone was asleep." Figuratively, being asleep can mean not paying attention, not being aware or conscious. Sometimes we say someone is "asleep at the wheel," not literally in a motor vehicle, but figuratively in a situation.

Good seed can be likened to wholesome intentions. What "enemies" (internal dynamics) in the personality sabotage our best intentions to be more fully the personality we ardently desire to be; to be more loving, find more peace, enjoy being alive, enjoy contributing to the lives of others as well as ourself.

Letting the wheat and weeds grow together until harvest can be likened to ripening the virtue of discernment. Discernment is wise judgment, sound choices, astute discriminations, sagacious knowing, intelligent commonsense, not only about decisions in the outer world, but about what goes on in our inner world. We are well advised to be awake, pay attention; stay alert, be discerning about the wheat and the weeds within our own personality; praying for insight, healing, transformation.

-32-
Treasure in a Field
The kingdom of heaven is like a treasure buried in a field, which a person finds and hides again, and out of joy goes and sells all that he has and buys that field. (Matthew 13:44)

Outer-world:
Isn't everyone looking for something so precious we'll do everything possible to make this treasure our own; whether an object, a relationship, an opportunity.

Inner-world:
A priceless psychological finding is a field or area of interest whereby one feels fulfilled, enthused, energized. This might be a hobby (avocation), a vocation, or a career. It is known that loss of interest is part of psychological depression. When Jesus says the kingdom of heaven is like buried treasure, he is saying that finding God transcends anything and everything one can yearn or long for; the "find" of a lifetime.

Drugs/chemicals are treasured for their ability to create a sense of well-being. More precious is knowing natural chemicals in the body react to thoughts, feelings, desires, hopes, expectations, fears, anxieties. Yes, psychological, behavioral factors and bodily chemicals are entwined.

Making choices:
Perhaps a most precious lifetime task is figuring out how we personally connect with the creative source of the universe so that even our body chemicals react to this creative hope.

Spiritually:
In this short parable, the person "finds and hides" the treasure before selling everything and buying the field. It is possible that sometime earlier in life, particularly puberty, adolescence, we have God-glimpses we may not have understood or known how to develop, but rediscover again later in life (midlife, perhaps), which we then invest in with our whole being.

The parable says, 'Out of joy' the person sells all and buys the field. Extraordinary! Not duty or responsibility, but joy is the treasure which jumpstarts the purchase. To what degree are we able to "buy into" the story of Jesus as cosmic companion, source of endless creative possibility, priceless personal treasure.

-33-
Pearl
The kingdom of heaven is like a merchant searching for fine pearls. When he finds a pearl of great price, he goes and sells all that he has and buys it. (Matthew 13:45-46)

Outer-world:
This is another Jesus story about selling all one has to buy one item; this time, a pearl. In everyday thinking, investing in this way would not be wise. A pearl, no matter how fine, is not enough to meet all one's needs. Jesus must be speaking figuratively.

Inner-world:
A pearl is a rich psychological image. A pearl is formed because of an irritant inside a live oyster far below the surface of the sea. The irritant is a parasite or a piece of shell that becomes lodged in the oyster's soft inner body. The oyster's body defends itself against the irritant by secreting "nacre" which coats the irritant layer upon layer with silky crystalline "nacre," and thus a beautiful pearl develops.

Being alive brings irritants, annoyances, aggravations, stresses small, large, huge. We do not consciously remember all events, yet, residues linger below consciousness in the waters of the unconscious, figuratively speaking; as body memory, cell memory, embodied memory; unconscious memory.

Humans need something like oyster's "nacre" to coat, cover, bathe psychological bruises and wounds in lustrous, radiant lovingness, removing the sting and pain of hurt. This parable tells us the kingdom of heaven is like a merchant searching for fine pearls. A merchant knows what he is looking for. Do we know what we really want? What we most long for? Might our ultimate desires lie in the depths of our being; borne from many of life's irritations and painfulness; where pearls of wisdom are waiting to be found in the layers and layers of wondrous mystery we are; including ancestry.

Making choices:

The pearl merchant sells all he has to buy the special pearl. If one's primary priority is seeking self-knowledge and God's healing, then time, effort, energy are needed to peel back layer upon layer of defense mechanisms to find irritants in the deepest levels of our being, so that others need not suffer our irritations.

Spiritually:

Surely, the psychological healing of humanity is the "pearl of great price" the price paid in the life, death, and resurrection of Jesus, who was eager for a new paradigm, the kingdom of heaven or God, to prevail on earth so that honesty, integrity, justice, mercy, respect, opportunity, encouragement, hope, compassion, wisdom, become greater and greater realities for more and more people. If personalities are full of habitual irritation, anger, exasperation, meanness, touchiness, frustration, crossness, impatience, neediness, fear, there is less room for creative responses to living with self and others.

-34-
Net

The kingdom of heaven is like a net thrown into the sea, which collects fish of every kind. When it is full they haul it ashore and sit down to put what is good into buckets. What is bad they throw away. (Matthew 13:47-48)

Outer-world:

This story is yet another kingdom of heaven parable; sifting-and-sorting between good and bad.

Inner-world:

Key words in this story are meaningful psychological images. Personality is like the sea: fluid, ever changing, flux. Thoughts, ideas, feelings, inklings, memories, are like fish swimming around in the body, person, personality. The net is gathering-in, catching-onto what floats and flows within one's being. A bucket is a receptable (receiver), the ability to contain, keep, maintain focus on certain elements going on inside oneself.

Each personality has its own ebb and flow. In early Christianity, two personality types were noted: active and contemplative. The active (extraverted) personality primarily uses energy in the outer world of happenings, events, and is also recharged with energy by dealing with the external world. Extraverts tend to process their thoughts by talking outwardly. The contemplative (introverted) personality uses and is recharged by the inner world of images, imagelessness, dreams, soul, dealing with self and humankind through prayer, relationship with the divine, expanding consciousness. Introverts tend to talk after processing their thoughts inwardly.

Both introversion and extraversion are necessary, essential and beneficial for humanity. Each personality is a mix of extraversion-introversion, though not usually a balanced mix. Spending too much in the inner world can become unhealthy introspection or self-absorption. Living only or mostly in the outer world, going and doing, can cause one to ignore inner equilibrium, one's core, one's center, one's deepest truth.

Making choices:

This parable concentrates on the net, hauling in the net, sitting down to sort through what has been collected in the net. This can be likened to reflecting on one's own experience: for example, the introversion-extraversion preference. This means noticing personal strengths and limitations stemming from one's particular inclination toward extraversion or introversion; looking at the dominant preference of parents, siblings; plus, cultural and religious influences toward extraversion or introversion in shaping one's own personality.

There are introversion-extraversion factors in friendships, with colleagues, romantic attractions, marriages, children; in the choices we make. Furthermore, in everyday practical living we display elements of introversion and extraversion.

<u>Spiritually:</u>

Was Jesus more introverted or extraverted? He seems to have been a well-integrated liberating mixture of both. We see extraversion in Jesus mingling with and teaching crowds, debating the learned of his day, interacting with strangers, concerned with the welfare of others especially the unfortunate. We see introversion in his going off by himself for extended times of prayer. After teaching a crowd he would dismiss the crowd to be with his disciples. During his agony in the garden, he needed the companionship of his disciples though they fell asleep, whereupon he had the inner strength to endure the ensuing horrific events alone.

-35-

Unforgiving Servant

The kingdom of heaven may be likened to a king who decided to settle accounts with his servants. When he began the accounting, a debtor was brought before him who owed him a huge amount. Since he had no way of paying it back, his master ordered him to be sold, along with his wife, his children, and all his property, in payment of the debt. At that, the servant fell down, did him homage, and said, 'Be patient with me, and I will pay you back in full" Moved with compassion the master of that servant let him go and forgave him the loan. When that servant had left, he found one of his fellow servants who owed him a much smaller amount. He seized him and started to choke him, demanding, "Pay back what you owe." Falling to his knees, his fellow servant begged him, "Be patient with me, and I will pay you back." But he refused. Instead, he had him put in prison until he paid back the debt. Now when his fellow servants saw what had happened, they were deeply disturbed, and went to their master and reported the whole affair. His master summoned him and said to him, "You wicked servant! I forgave you your entire debt because you begged me to. Should you not have had pity on your fellow servant, as I had pity on you?" Then in anger his master handed him over to the torturers until he should pay back the whole debt. So will my heavenly Father do to you, unless each of you forgives his brother from his heart. (Matthew 18:23-35)

<u>Outer-world:</u>

There is mental-physical harshness and cruelty in this parable: threatening to sell the servant, his wife, children, property, followed by the same servant seizing and choking another, and anger so great that torturers are called in. What is going on here?

Inner-world:

Should we regard the servant forgiven a huge debt a picture of us when we forget to be grateful? Is he a reminder shocking us into not being forgetful, clueless, ungrateful wretches? Maybe. Yet there is another plausible explanation for his behavior: institutional servitude.

Master-to-servant is top-down forgiveness of debt. Servant-to-servant dynamics are different, for they include psychological scars and wounds of internalized inferiority, inherent in a system where the master has the option of carrying out his threat to sell servant, wife and children (slavery). A "less than" status creates rage in the person devalued, treated as a commodity, and this bitterness is then displaced onto a fellow servant with a smaller debt in this story, who is a safe target for anger and bullying because he has no power. Such behavior is labeled "displacement" in psychology, and is a human mechanism of taking one's frustration and bitterness caused by other sources, and inflicting stress on someone who likely cannot hurt you back. This psychological mechanism is present when viciousness is perpetrated by some members on other members within the same disenfranchised group.

Making choices:

This parable may be exposing systemic evil and its reverberations when a group of people is enslaved, made to feel second-rate, taken advantage of while others have power and privilege. The plot reinforces Jesus' enduring insight that a society or culture where the kingdom of God is present and evolving must be built on an attitude of all people being respected, working together, serving each other; co-operating.

Spiritually:

Teacher-storyteller Jesus uses hyperbole (exaggeration), contrast, tension, paradox, open-endedness, in the tales he tells, which makes us think, wonder about and question our assumptions, our behaviors, the collective systems in which we live.

At first glance, this story seems to be about a deplorable, ungrateful, mean-spirited, crass servant. From a broader perspective, however, this appears to be a dominoeffect story of social/cultural injustice which lacks respect for some, therefore inflicting

pain and savagery, creating anger and violence, and requiring many shades of for-
giveness to heal the situation.

For nuanced, multi-faceted understanding of shades of forgiveness, read the simply
profound and profoundly simple book, Don't Forgive Too Soon: Extending the
Two Hands That Heal, *by Dennis Linn, Sheila Fabricant Linn, Matthew Linn.*

-36-
Workers and Wages

"The kingdom of heaven is like a landowner who went out at dawn
to hire laborers for his vineyard. After agreeing with them for the
usual daily wage, he sent them into his vineyard. Going out about
nine o'clock, he saw others standing idle in the marketplace, and
he said to them, 'You too go into my vineyard, and I will give you
what is just.' So they went off. He went out again around noon, and
around three o'clock, and did likewise. Going out about five
o'clock, he found others standing around, and said to them, 'Why
do you stand here idle all day?' They answered, 'Because no one
has hired us.'

He said to them, 'You too go into my vineyard.' When it was
evening the owners of the vineyard said to his foreman, 'Summon
the laborers and give them their pay, beginning with the last and
ending with the first.' When those who had started about five
o'clock came, each received the usual daily wage. So when the first
came, they thought that they would receive more, but each of them
also got the usual wage. And on receiving it they grumbled against
the landowner, saying, 'These last ones worked only one hour, and
you have made them equal to us, who bore the day's burden and
the heat.' He said to one of them in reply, 'My friend, I am not
cheating you. Did you not agree with me for the usual daily wage?
Take what is yours and go. What if I wish to give this last one the
same as you? Am I not free to do as I wish with my own money?
Are you envious because I am generous? Thus, the last will be first,
and the first will be last." (Matthew 20:1-16)

Outer-world:

The vineyard owner can be as generous with his money as he wants, so long as he does not pay anyone less than originally agreed upon. But it is not clear why he returns to the marketplace four times in one day after hiring his first workers. Perhaps he does not approve of idleness. Or he has calculated his vineyard will prosper more if worked properly that very day, no matter the cost, which still does not explain why he overpays the later workers.

Inner-world:

Like the vineyard owner, we need "help" every hour of the day. Alone, our task is beyond our capacity to deal with fears, anxieties, angers, addictions, lethargies, hopelessness, guilt, shame, worry, difficult relationships, which clog the brain and sap energy. Perhaps "the last will be first, and the first will be last" is part of recognizing that often the last thing we want to do is again deal with aspects of our personality that are upset, frightened, angry, or otherwise stressed.

When the vineyard owner asks the idle laborers, 'Why do you stand here idle all day?' They answer, 'Because no one has hired us,' possibly alludes to parts of the personality unaware of the need to seek grace daily, hourly, moment-by-moment.

Making choices:

The vineyard owner seems to understand his situation and what is needed. Like him, we must make practical decisions taking care of ourself as well as others, in our circumstances, our sphere of influence, our corner of the world, especially our inner world where we really live.

Spiritually:

The vineyard owner knows he needs help and more help, as the day passes, growing older. This is praying unceasingly. The parable may also reassure those who do not search spiritually until late in life, "late in the day," that their efforts are no less worthwhile.

And finally, Jesus' kingdom of God where "the last will be first, and the first will be last" can be about re-arranging priorities about what we do with our time, our energy, as we grow spiritually, as we mature, as we evolve into harvesting a fruitful existence for oneself and others.

-37-
Two Sons

A man had two sons. He came to the first and said, "Son, go out and work in the vineyard today." He said in reply, "I will not," but afterwards he changed his mind and went. The man came to the other son and gave the same order. He said in reply, "Yes, sir," but did not go. Which of the two did his father's will? (Matthew 21:28-32)

Outer-world:

This is an example of "actions speak louder than words;" what we do counts more than mere lip-service.

Inner-world:

Maybe each son in the parable answers too quickly, and upon reflection reverses his swift decision. This story might demonstrate not knowing one's own mind, blind obedience, impulsive compliance, lack of independent judgment, shallow assessment of a situation where coercion, manipulation, authoritarian influence may be present, or unexamined reactionary opposition, habitual defiance, rebellious tendency, anger or fear.

Likely, every person remembers saying "yes" or "no" too fast, too automatically. If this is a pesky pattern in our personality, we need to wonder what makes us rush to judgment. What pushes or pulls us in one direction or another?

Making choices:

There is always the importance of choosing, judging, deciding, which the two sons do in this story though in opposite ways. On what basis do we come to conclusions? To what degree do we rely on group-think—aspects of today's social mindset—experts or expertise, religious or family tradition, childhood conditioning, logical deduction, memory of past experiences, feelings, intuitions, inklings, impressions, bodily reactions. Perhaps these and more play a role in decision-making.

Humans shape the world with the large and small choices we make, which is both an awesome opportunity and an overwhelming responsibility.

Spiritually:

When Jesus tells this parable, he is under pressure; his spiritual authority is being questioned by people with religious clout. In this stressful encounter, Jesus uses a parable. We don't know whether he formed this parable on the spot in the heat of the moment, whether it occurred to him earlier, or he heard it from someone else. What seems significant is the importance he places on figurative understanding for profound, penetrating insight.

This tense episode ends with Jesus saying the tax collectors and prostitutes (religious outcasts) are entering the kingdom of God before the people who are questioning him (religious leaders). Do we know what is "taxing" to us in our inner world that spills over into the outer world thus "taxing" others? In what ways do we sometimes "prostitute" our integrity? Which of our "religious" attitudes help or hinder us?

-38-

No Wedding Garment

The kingdom of heaven may be likened to a king who gave a wedding feast for his son. He dispatched his servants to summon the invited guests to the feast, but they refused to come. A second time he sent other servants, saying, 'Tell those invited: Behold, I have prepared my banquet, my calves and fattened cattle are killed, and everything is ready: come to the feast.' Some ignored the invitation and went away, one to his farm, another to his business. The rest laid hold of his servants, mistreated them, and killed them. The king was enraged and sent his troops, destroyed those murderers, and burned their city. Then he said to his servants. 'The feast is ready, but those who were invited were not worthy to come. Go out, therefore, into the main roads and invite to the feast whomever you find.' The servants went out into the streets and gathered all they found, bad and good alike, and the hall was filled with guests. But when the king came in to meet the guests he saw a man there not dressed in a wedding garment. He said to him, 'My friend, how is it that you came in here without a wedding garment?' But he was reduced to silence. Then the king said to his attendants, 'Bind his hands and feet, and cast him into the darkness outside, where there will be wailing and grinding of teeth.' Many are invited, but few are chosen. (Matthew 22:2-14)

<u>Outer-world:</u>

In this parable there is mistreatment, being enraged, destroying, killing, binding hands and feet, casting into darkness, wailing and grinding of teeth. Why such violence over wedding invitations?

<u>Inner-world:</u>

Psychologically, a wedding feast can symbolize coming together, integration of complementary elements in the personality. Right-hemisphere intuitive, spiral, simultaneous, affective embodied experience; left-hemisphere: analytical, linear, logical, abstracted experience. In depth psychology, these qualities are sometimes referred to as feminine and masculine elements in the personality. They can also be considered neurological pathways shaped by sex-roles of females and males over countless generations; eons of time.

It is now known the right hemisphere forms first in the fetus brain. The right hemisphere deals with ambiguity. The left hemisphere searches for certainty. The right hemisphere embraces mystery. The left hemisphere solves problems. Obviously, individuals and cultures live more fully, more wisely, when both sides of the brain are valued. Life is compromised when one side is preferred exclusively over the other.

In depth psychology, in literature, in dreams, in mystical traditions, marriage represents uniting, joining, fusing, mixing, bonding, blending; consummating personal experience with overall existence.

<u>Making choices:</u>

Many are invited, but few are chosen. This is a story about choice: invited guests who choose not to "come to the feast," because of other priorities, and those who do choose to show up, including one individual thrown out for being improperly dressed.

The improperly dressed person suggests outer demeanor, what is worn on the outside, clothing as external behavior. This implies that what we "do," can make us unsuitable to celebrate the fullness of life; to feast on life itself. Behavior matters in quality of life: obviously avoiding some behaviors, and putting on other behaviors, makes a difference.

The violence in this story may portray what we do to ourself when we do not come to the spiritual feast Jesus brought to earth for struggling humanity, but instead, for whatever reasons, try to live by our own efforts alone.

<u>Spiritually:</u>

Pretend Jesus is inadvertently speaking of brain-hemispheres in this parable. Being an astute observer of humanity, his marriage parable alludes to what brings forth new life. Feminine-masculine elements are needed to create babies. Marriage symbolizes potential for new life whether "the marriage" is physical, psychological, or spiritual.

Jesus himself shows that intuitive insight (right-hemisphere) as well as penetrating analysis (left-hemisphere) bring revelation, enlightened understanding. He knew human nature, and in this story metaphorically expresses as marriage some of what science began learning fifty-plus years ago with split-brain research. That is, the fullness of life humans bring forth when interpreting experience with the perspectives of both sides of the brain.

-39-

Ten Bridesmaids

The kingdom of heaven will be like ten bridesmaids who took their lamps and went out to meet the bridegroom. Five of them were foolish and five were wise. The foolish ones, when taking their lamps, brought no oil with them, but the wise brought flasks of oil with their lamps. Since the bridegroom was long delayed, they all became drowsy and fell asleep. At midnight, there was a cry. 'Behold, the bridegroom! Come out to meet him!' Then all those bridesmaids got up and trimmed their lamps. The foolish ones said to the wise, 'Give us some of your oil, for our lamps are going out.' But the wise ones relied, 'No, for there may not be enough for us and you. Go instead to the merchants and buy some for yourselves.' While they went off to buy it, the bridegroom came and those who were ready went into the wedding feast with him. Then the door was locked. Afterwards the other bridesmaids came and said, 'Lord, Lord, open the door for us!' But he said in reply, 'Amen, I say to you, I do not know you.' Therefore, stay awake, for you know neither the day nor the hour.'" (Matthew 25:1-13)

<u>Outer-world:</u>

Jesus' parables were woven from every day experiences and customs. For example, the parable of the foolish bridesmaids who did not have enough oil for their lamps may have been based on actual marriage customs at the time of Jesus. In the arranged marriages of his day, there were three stages leading to marriage: engagement, betrothal, marriage. Engagement took place in childhood when parents matched the children for marriage; betrothal was when the couple reached marriageable age; the wedding took place a year after betrothal. If the bridegroom lived away from the area, there was no saying when he would arrive for the wedding. This is the likely background for Jesus' parable of the waiting bridesmaids.

Inner-world:

The parable says, "Stay awake." Does this mean we are to never sleep, which is an impractical, unlivable suggestion? Jesus came to give us abundant life, not outrageous suggestions.

"Stay awake" psychologically, is about being aware, mindful, conscious. Lamps and oil for lamps are about light, wanting to be enlightened, wanting to be able to "see," to not be "in the dark," to have "insight" about who we are and who we can become. It's about being able to "see" what goes on in our personality.

As a wedding story, which represents uniting, bringing together, joining, we may want to get our personality, our life, "together," which happens only if we put energy (oil) into looking for, searching, questing, waiting for Spirit, God, our Higher Power.

Making choices:

Our duty, responsibility, the attitude we need, is to be ready, prepared, to "see" (lamps full of oil) and "listen" to what psycho-spiritual insights await us every hour and day. Other people (the bridesmaids with enough oil) cannot always give us the wisdom we need. We must foster this in our own personality.

Spiritually:

It is foolish not to expect practical wisdom coming to us. Otherwise, we have an uninspired existence, remaining in the dark, unprepared for nudges, hints and clues, inspirations, whispers, intimations of caring love available to us.

We may want specific answers to specific questions. We do not know the timing involved. God's actions often seem tardy from the human side of life. We get impatient, but do not know all the issues, circumstances involved, or the lessons required for us to be united to who we really are, and our meaning and purpose. Who one is and what one is about is ultimately molded, shaped, formed by the relationship one does or does not have with Love (the bridegroom) the source and object of our most profound yearnings and longings. Jesus was in love with that Love. Jesus the Christ is that Love.

-40-

Human Need

When the Son of Man comes in his glory, and all the angels with him, he will sit upon his glorious throne, and all the nations will be assembled before him. And he will separate them one from another, as a shepherd separates the sheep from the goats. He will place the sheep on his right and the goats on his left. Then the king will say to those on his right, 'Come, you are blessed by my Father. Inherit the kingdom prepared for you from the foundation of the world. For I was hungry and you gave me food, I was thirsty and you gave me drink, a stranger and you welcomed me, naked and you clothed me, ill and you cared for me, in prison and you visited me.' Then the righteous will answer him and say, 'Lord, when did we see you hungry and feed you, or thirsty and give you drink? When did we see you a stranger and welcome you, or naked and clothe you? When did we see you ill or in prison, and visit you?' And the king will say to them in reply, 'Amen, I say to you, whatever you did for one of these least brothers of mine, you did for me.' Then he will say to those on his left, 'Depart from me, you accursed, into the eternal fire prepared for the devil and his angels. For I was hungry and you gave me no food, I was thirsty and you gave me no drink, a stranger and you gave me no welcome, naked and you gave me no clothing, ill and in prison, and you did not care for me.' Then they will answer and say, 'Lord, when did we see you hungry or thirsty or a stranger or naked or ill or in prison, and not minister to your needs?' He will answer them, 'Amen, I say to you, what you did not do for one of these least ones, you did not do for me.' And these will go off to eternal punishment, but the righteous to eternal life. (Matthew 25:31-46)

Outer-world:

In this story, sheep and the "right" side are preferred over goats and the "left" side. Sheep are usually thought to be docile and follow the herd; goats are more independent and go their own way. Is docility always the best course of action; is independence always best?

"Right" also means correct. "Left" can mean not used, not needed; "left-over, left-behind." In this story, the "righteous" go on to eternal life. Is this parable really about sheep or goats, right or left? Likely, human need is what is emphasized in the story.

Inner-world:

Psychologically speaking, we are all needy. We have parts of our personality that are hungry, thirsty, naked, a stranger, ill, or imprisoned. We may feel chronically unfulfilled, empty. We can also thirst, feel parched, dried-up, bored, in need of refreshing, renewing ideas, outlook, perspective, mindset, hopefulness, interest, enthusiasm. We perhaps feel a stranger, apart from, not known or accepted, lonely. We can feel naked and vulnerable, weak, powerless, unprotected, frightened. We may be mentally, emotionally confused, overwhelmed, desperate, despairing, paralyzed or out-of-control. We might feel imprisoned, held-down, controlled, constricted, confined, in need of liberation from what binds us to distressed mental/emotional states of being.

Do we stubbornly assume we alone, independently, willfully, can make our lives fulfilling, or do we in a more docile way realize we need help, guidance, caring assistance from The Source beyond?

Making choices:

This parable is surely a story about right conduct, compassionate priorities, helping those in need, our duty to others and their plight. It is surely also a story about our own neediness; our need to be open to our own positive and negative traits and qualities that need our attention, and doing the "right" thing for self and others.

Spiritually:

Christ Jesus, teacher and healer of the soul, the human personality, was himself human, knowing well human neediness. Each personality is part of the human condition, for better or worse.

Christians have in Christ a cosmic caregiver who has opened doors to human potential. Parables are part of his life-changing legacy.

Closing Comment

Below is a saying of Jesus which at first glance seems outrageous and disjointed. What might a fourfold perspective make of this?

If anyone comes to me without hating his father and mother, wife and children, brothers and sisters, and even his own life, he cannot

be my disciple. Whoever does not carry his own cross and come after me cannot be my disciple. Which of you wishing to construct a tower does not first sit down and calculate the cost to see if there is enough for its completion? Otherwise, after laying the foundation and finding himself unable to finish the work the onlookers should laugh at him and say, 'This one began to build but did not have the resources to finish. Or what king marching into battle would not first sit down and decide whether with ten thousand troops he can successfully oppose another king advancing upon him with twenty thousand troops? But if not, while he is still far away, he will send a delegation to ask for peace terms. In the same way, every one of you who does not renounce all his possessions cannot be my disciple. (Luke 14:26-33)

Outer-world:

If people strictly follow the beginning and ending sentences of this comment with simplistic understanding, everyone will have the goal of being destitute and homeless, hating one's very existence, having no family ties.

Inner-world:

One's own cross can be one's own personality with it many tensions, opposites, contradictions, and potentials. In order to evolve into the personality one can potentially become, making one's unique contributions may well require being stretched beyond family bonds, family ways of doing and being.

As for possessions, in depth psychology it is known a personality can be "possessed," controlled by certain emotions, moods, thoughts, concerns, labeled "complexes" which mildly or profoundly interfere with one's best intentions, and how we want our personality to be and do. It's as if some ideas or feelings take root in the personality and won't let go; they keep us psychologically blocked, prevent us from being psychologically free, liberated, wholly who we can be. Do we know what "possesses" us?

Making choices:

The middle of Jesus' comment is about analyzing, assessing, gauging, estimating the cost of building a tower or the number of soldiers needed in battle. These are examples of calculating what it takes to responsibly make practical decisions, well-thought-out choices. Are we free enough inside to have such clarity?

<u>Spiritually:</u>

We are told great crowds were traveling with Jesus when he turned to them and made this unsettling comment. Had he discerned the crowd did not know what they were getting into by associating with him: how their families might disapprove of or disown them, how their own priorities would change, how resistances and urgings within their personalities would need attention, growth, development. Is he painting a worst-case scenario, or reminding them that struggle is a necessary part of creative change? Jesus' saying is not disjointed, for indeed, a topic emerges, which is how limited ego-me-I relates to creative possibility; building a tower, seeking a higher perspective. Soldiers in the story might suggest interior conflict, doing battle with oneself. Overall, the top priority of a Jesus disciple (learner, pupil, student, friend, companion, lover) is to be willing to carry one's own cross, the totality of one's personality, into becoming a vessel of prayer and grace.

~~~~

Francine gave a copy of Dee's interpretation of Jesus' parables to longtime clients Kelly and Paul, still in therapy seeking to improve their marriage. Dee felt gratified that Francine valued her comments on the parables enough to share the material with the couple.

Monique remarked, "Many parables repeat themes with slight difference." Monique laughed at herself, "Only I know my meaning, my understanding. But why so many parables?"

Dee replied, "Why did Jesus tell so many parables? He was speaking to different people on different occasions, teaching lessons in various situations. The stories were written down by different authors in the four gospels. The human condition requires countless distinctions and differentiations. I assume his discernments were many, especially suited for whomever he was telling a specific story. This seems real to me.

"Just as each of us has different needs on different days, or even moment by moment. We need constant contact with the MORE of the universe to live well. For a meaningful existence, humans require ongoing relationship with the Life Force, the Life Source, which is always seeking us."

Estelle tells Dee how she and Dexter have occasional telephone conversations on Dee's fourfold explications. Dexter has high regard for

Dee's easy-to-understand figurative insights. Moreover, Estelle's gazing love affair with the icon of the Virgin of Vladimir remains. The nearly 900-year-old-icon, also known as "Our Lady of Tenderness," increases in Estelle's imagination; the painting's emotional tenderness lives inside Estelle. The icon child's eyes seem like Estelle's eyes. And Estelle never takes her eyes off Mary, human Mary, named Mother of God, cosmic feminine. Words cannot adequately express the tenderness, the gentle strength of this painting alive in Estelle, for she keeps it readily available, and sometimes sits with it.

Estelle uses the word *imagination* to describe ways in which she experiences mental pictures in sleeptime dreams; dream images. She also deals with mental images in Gospel stories in the Spiritual Exercises of Ignatius of Loyola, and now, with mental imagery in gazing at the icon of cosmic Mary, mother of Jesus.

Estelle knows there is mental imagery in daydreaming, whether creative or destructive. She remembers the difference between phantasy and fantasy. Phantasy is spontaneous. Fantasy is more willful, the product of human effort. Estelle is wonder-struck about this image-making capacity in us.

Dee is satisfied with her fourfold "take" on Jesus' parables, even if only she benefits from the extrapolations, for she's been sitting with the parables, allowing symbols, Jesus' metaphoric utterances, to penetrate her being. Sitting with the parables, paying attention to her interior reactions, continues to bring Dee understanding, awareness, which is carried forth in the next novel of this series, *Sit With It.*

ACKNOWLEDGMENTS

Special thanks to Maureen Lumley, PhD, who connected the author with Jennifer Leigh Selig, PhD, publisher of Empress Publications.

www.ingramcontent.com/pod-product-compliance
Lightning Source LLC
Chambersburg PA
CBHW060642260626

47161CB00008B/2966